I0831656

THE CHRISTMAS MURDERS

The Christmas Murders
Published by Sweaty Boy Publishing

ISBN (Hardback): 979-8-9938431-0-0
ISBN (eBook): 979-8-9938431-1-7

Cover design: Everett Wood
Printed in the United States of America
First Edition 2025
1 2 3 4 5 6 7 8 9 10
12/01/25

ZERO

Catherine Fidelia Dryden was nine years old the winter night she first saw Lilly Edith Cooper from her window-sill overlooking the drive at Stratford Hall. The frost had drawn lace across the glass, and through it Catherine spied a small figure at the gate—bare-headed, clutching a limp rag-doll against the wind. Snow had begun to fall in earnest, whitening the hedgerows and steps.

"She's quite underdressed for the weather we're having—so impractical, these factory types," Catherine murmured, half to herself, repeating one of her father's expressions. She'd often overheard him at dinner railing against the working poor—how they squandered their wages on beer and bread, those "two pillars of poverty." Catherine, bright but ignorant of such matters, knew little of the mills beyond her father's complaints about idle foremen and broken machines.

Down below, Lilly Cooper—a child scarcely older than Catherine herself and employed at one of the Spinning Jennies—was beating her small fists upon the great oak doors, crying out between sobs that she was ill, that something dreadful had happened at the factory. Catherine crept to the top of the stairs to listen, her breath fogging the banister.

One of the maids, Abby, had answered the door and stood speaking softly to the girl, whose tears streamed down a face pinched blue with cold. Abby disappeared for a moment, then returned with a crust of bread wrapped in a towel. The girl asked, almost whispered, if she might stay the night by the kitchen fire.

Before the maid could reply, Catherine's young voice came brightly down the stairwell: "Absolutely not! Father would never approve, Abby."

A silence followed—heavy, mortified. Then the door closed with a sigh, and Lilly was gone, swallowed by the white dark of the evening.

She was found the next morning by a paper-merchant from Manchester, lying stiff beside the lane that bordered the estate, her doll frozen fast in one small hand. The news travelled quickly through Werseby, though it was never spoken of at the Hall. Lord Dryden never knew, or perhaps never cared to know, what had transpired.

Catherine carried the secret into her womanhood like a stone sewn into her heart. Each Christmas, when the air grew sharp and the servants lit the fires in every hearth, she would pause by the great door and listen for the faint sound of knocking beneath the wind. No apparition ever came—only the memory, pale as frost on glass, of a child who had once begged for warmth and been refused it.

ONE

"Do you know what money is?"

The two gentlemen seated opposite Mr. Levi Jonathan Bairstow blinked at him, as if he had asked whether gravity took sugar in its tea.

"Nuffin!—absolutely *bleedin'* nuffin!" squealed Mr. L. J. Bairstow in his aged, asthmatic manner, half-giggle, half-wheeze. "Haw! The buffoonery of it all! The whole rickety enterprise!"

"Wha' you mean, *nuffin*, Levi?" inquired young Sam Hedge, clerk and general drudge to the establishment, his face arranged in that same dim confusion that so endeared him to his employer. His brother Adoniram, seated beside him, nodded in earnest secondment.

Mr. Bairstow, with the air of a man about to deliver a lecture to Parliament itself, reached into the interior of his shabby velvet jacket and drew forth a handkerchief of brilliant blue. Into this he trumpeted a noise like a dying tuba, then immediately followed it with a wheezing chuckle and a hearty gulp from his tankard of ale—an act which nearly proved his undoing. The Hedge brothers leaned forward in alarm as the old fellow spluttered, gasped, and thumped his chest.

Having survived his own enthusiasm, Mr. Bairstow straightened himself and glared triumphantly at the brothers, as though his near asphyxiation had somehow proved his point.

"Money, my sons," he began, raising a stubby forefinger, "is *an arbitrary symbol of wealth*—hah! there's a phrase for ye—that the banks dream up on the ruddy spot!"

He raised both hands now and made his favorite gesture: waggling two sets of inverted commas in the air, a performance he believed gave philosophical weight to any phrase he quoted.

The Hedge brothers blinked, those identical brown eyes glazed in good-natured incomprehension. They were mirror images—tall, fair, and freckled—each dressed in the respectable attire their master had paid for, and each entirely innocent of the higher mysteries of finance. Mr. Bairstow, being of short, stout, and round persuasion (indeed, resembling a pudding given human features), had hired them to supply the dignity he lacked in stature.

"You lads work hard for me—bloody hard," he continued, "and I remunerate you handsomely—too handsomely, some would say." (In truth, Mr. Bairstow paid them about a third of the going rate, but the twins were too grateful, or too dim, to notice.) "The wage you deposit each week is earned by the *sweat of thy brow*—real spoil won in return for real effort, time, and labour."

He paused to sip his ale again, and the brothers nodded dutifully, as though listening to a sermon they did not quite understand but dared not interrupt.

"But the Bank of England," he resumed, with a glare of righteous indignation, "*neither spins nor toils*! Yet it conjures riches from the very ether, and calls it progress. The whole lot of 'em, sittin' in their marble halls, pullin' coin out o' thin blessed air! Think on it, lads—think hard!"

The Hedge brothers exchanged a glance that implied a mutual agreement to think on it later, if ever.

Mr. Bairstow sat back, red-faced and triumphant, and wiped his brow. "The buffoonery," he muttered again, shaking his head. "A nation of clerks and conjurers, that's what we've become. And when the whole house of cards tumbles down, they'll call it an *unforeseen calamity!*"

He leaned forward once more, his eyes gleaming with that peculiar delight known only to men who enjoy their own outrage. "Mark me, boys," he said, tapping the table with a fat finger, "money ain't gold, it ain't silver, it ain't even paper. It's *faith.* And faith, once lost, is dearer than any crown."

There was a brief silence. Sam Hedge, after due consideration, ventured, "So… shall we still take it, then, sir?"

Mr. Bairstow regarded him as one might a particularly disappointing turnip. Then he sighed, leaned back, and said, "Aye, Sam. Take it. Spend it. But never *believe* in it."

He tried again, this time with more animation and a sort of evangelical quickening in his tone.

"If *you*, Sam," he said, wagging a finger heavy with a ring that had long ago lost its stone, "should go to the bank and request a loan, that loan is not money the bank has in its possession—not a farthing of it! Nay, it is money the bank *creates*, *ex nihilo*, out o' the void, as the Lord made the heavens and the earth! Only, in this case, the creation is accompanied by interest—and a prayer that you default. For when you do, the bank reclaims not illusion but substance—real estate! And that, lads, is what *property* is—estate that is *real!*"

He slapped the table so that the mugs rattled.

"Land," he continued, drawing out the word with reverence, "is real *wealff*—the only wealth worth havin'—for which the bankers lust as Ahab lusted after Naboth's vineyard! And that, my sons, is real power—the power of God Himself—the 'power to get wealff,' as Solomon spake in Deuteronomy or some such blessed corner of Scripture."

The Hedge brothers stared, glassy-eyed, as if their employer were unveiling a divine mystery rather than a crooked balance sheet.

"Money," he thundered, "is *nuffin*—and yet it may cost us *everyffin!* Miss a single installation—yes, I said *installation*—toward the loan that the goodly men of the Bank of England have granted us, and lo! the Law shall descend upon L. J. Bairstow Textiles Co. like the Angel of Death in Egypt, and reclaim the firstborn of every blessed spool and spindle. Therefore, lads, the mules must operate uninterrupted—day and bloody night! I want sheets over the windows, locks on the privy, and fingers nimble as sparrows. Is that clear?"

The Hedges nodded, chastened and bewildered.

"Good. Now, regarding the unfortunate circumstance of young Til'—his passing was a tragic affair, to be sure, but the work must go on. Will Mr. John Henry Hill of the Bank of England observe the cessation of a single drop of ink to his ledgers on account o' the death of a little orphan rat? Neither shall they, neither shall I! Dust thou art, and to dust thou shalt return—but the inventory must remain upright!"

At this, Adoniram Hedge half-whispered, his conscience quivering like a leaf, "Levi, William Avondale has intimated that some fault lies with the way our—"

"Nonsense!" bellowed Mr. Bairstow, striking the table so hard that a crust of ale leapt from his mug. "Avondale shall be rebuked! I'll have Constable Blackwood deal with that meddlesome fool before the day's end. The beams have been traversed a thousand times and shall be another thousand! We've neither the time nor the foolishness to repair what needeth not repair. *Let not him that girdeth his loins faint in the day of adversity!*"

"Right-o, Levi—right-o!" Sam applauded eagerly. "Adonyram 'ere don't like it much when Flick come out, but spare the rod, spoil the factory, says I!"

He was referring, of course, to his rod—a polished length of hickory about the height of a child and the width of a man's thumb. "Flick'll see my loves back to the Mule Jenny's—I promise you that, Levi!"

"I should ruddy hope so, lads. I should ruddy hope so," sighed Mr. Bairstow, wiping his brow with the blue handkerchief, as if the burden of empire rested on his damp forehead.

And with that, mugs were drained, a barkeep was underpaid, and paths were made back to L. J. Bairstow Textiles Co.—where the air was thick with lint and hymnless labour. Before dusk, a boy was dispatched through the sooty lanes carrying letters of instruction regarding the matter of Mr. William Zachariah Avondale, directed to one Constable Hiram Walter Blackwood—a man whose idea of justice, like Bairstow's own, was ever for sale by the pint.

TWO

"A wee bit to the left, Catherine," whispered Father Flynn, raising his hand like a choirmaster. "Lead 'em now—steady—there!"

Snah-boom! went the flint hammer—spark, flash, and smoke. Thirty feet ahead, a pheasant gave one indignant flap, then plummeted into the grass with a sound like a dropped pillow. The dogs tore off, yapping in ecstasy.

"Saint Joseph preserve us! You're a crack-shot, Cat!" cried Father Flynn, capering a little jig, his cassock flapping like laundry on the line.

His celebration was abruptly interrupted by a far-off roar from the hedgerow.

"Ah, the divil choke ye himself, Flynn!" bawled a voice both ancient and indignant.

"Is that you, my lost little sheep?" shouted Flynn, hand to brow, squinting toward the commotion.

Catherine Fidelia Dryden laughed under her breath. From the moving tangle of green there issued a clatter, a curse, and then the bent figure of Mr. Isaac Benjamin Digby—a keeper of sheep, goats, and grievances.

"Diggy," as he called himself, was a sight to sober the saints: a tattered top-hat perched on wisps of grey, a filthy scarlet tunic from some forgotten regiment, and a pair of waders patched more than worn. Across his chest hung a confusion of straps and pouches, clinking faintly like small ghosts of campaign medals.

The villagers counted him harmless, if eccentric; strangers took him for a prophet or a scarecrow that had learned to speak.

"Ahh—blast yer blessed cannon, Father," he wheezed, hacking through the briar. "Boomin' and bangin' and all me kids boltin'—baaah!—like Gabriel come blowin' down t'field! Sheep's no stomach for salvation, no they bain't! Boom once more an' I'll stick ye in the Book o' Revelations meself!"

Father Flynn laughed so heartily he was forced to remove his hat and mop his curly white head. "She didn't hit ye, did she, Isaac?" he called, still chuckling. "Though truth told, I can't say ye'd notice the difference!"

"Hit? *Hit?*" cried Diggy, blinking owlishly. "Nay, but near 'nuff, Father! Bullet went singin' past me ear like an angel that's forgot the words!"

Catherine lowered her musket, pressing the stock against her stomach and pulling off one glove to tame a rebellious curl. Beneath her grey hunting hat, dark eyes scanned the field for the hounds. The picture she made—poised, calm, and bright against the moor—was enough to make a poet bite his quill.

Miss Dryden, only daughter of Lord Dryden of Stratford Hall, lived in that curious household where the musket and missal shared a shelf. With no mother and few companions save the priest, she spent her days on horseback, at prayer, or in pursuit of game. She could quote Virgil before breakfast and shoot supper before dusk.

"Saints alive," muttered Diggy, leaning on his stick. "She's a witch-shot, that one. Devil's aim in a saint's face. World's turned widdershins, it has—girls shootin', priests dancin', goats prayin' to be mutton!"

"Hush now," said Flynn, wagging a finger at him. "She's God's own marksman, that's what she is. 'He teacheth my hands to war, and my fingers to fight,' says the Psalmist!"

Catherine smiled. "If the Lord arms the righteous, Father, I trust He'll reload for them as well."

Flynn gave a hearty chuckle, while Diggy, unconvinced, muttered something about angels duckin' for cover.

Of all the women north of York, none inspired such dread or devotion as Catherine Fidelia Dryden. The sons of neighboring families approached her like pilgrims and returned like casualties—tongue-tied, heartsick, and, on one memorable occasion, limping. The fathers blamed her upbringing, the mothers blamed her mind, and both blamed Father Flynn.

"Mark me," Diggy croaked as he turned to go, "one day she'll shoot the moon out the sky, and then where'll we hang the clouds?"

"Then Heaven will be brighter for it," said Flynn cheerfully.

And Catherine, smoothing her glove and watching the hounds return with their feathery prize, replied with a spark in her eye, "If Heaven flies low enough, Mr. Digby, it may take its chances."

"And now ye've gone and dunnit, Gid Flynn," croaked Diggy, stamping one boot in the mud. "Now ye've proper dunnit. Bubs is bolted off, he has! Gone like a puff o' brimstone, and me legs not fit to chase a dream. Will take Diggy rest o' the day, maybe two, to find 'im again. Devil choke ye kindly, Father Flynn!"

Father Gideon Timothy Flynn only laughed, that soft, priestly chuckle that sounded halfway between forgiveness and mischief. "I'll help you find Bubs, Isaac—don't you take on so. Lady Dryden," he said, turning to Catherine, "I'll relieve you of that musket, if you please. Up to the house with you now, and we'll resume this lesson come the morrow."

Catherine laughed, handing him the musket—her father's pride, polished and deadly. "Don't you lose that bird, Father," she said, eyes sparkling. "I mean to show Daddy who the best shot in Stratford Hall is now!"

Flynn accepted the weapon with mock solemnity and slung it over his shoulder. He cast a glance at Diggy, then back to Catherine, then once more to Diggy, his blue eyes glinting. "Have you been at the bottle, Isaac Digby? You're pale as a winding sheet."

"Boomin'," answered Diggy, lowering his voice to a conspiratorial rasp. "And the new ghost. Been puttin' the flock to fright, it has. Scared the Jesus right out o' Diggy last night, it did. Couldn't sleep till mornin' light. Was restin' now, peaceful like, till you come a-boomin', and I thought 'twer the ghost again, trumpet and all."

Flynn's expression softened. "A ghost, is it? Well, I've known a few, and none could stand a bit o' stew. Why don't you come by me cottage, Isaac? Have a meal, sit by the fire, and tell me about this spirit of yours."

"Diggy don't like chairs," said the old man, shaking his head so that his battered hat slipped down over one eye.

"Does Diggy like a warm potato stew?" pressed Flynn, "with a touch o' beef and buttered bread besides? We'll find your Bubs first, and then you'll sup with me. I'll even let you choose the chair least offensive to your dignity."

At the name of Bubs, Diggy grew solemn. The creature was a large ram with a white crown-shaped tuft upon his head, and Diggy, having declared it a sign of royalty, had spared him the butcher's knife years ago. He now referred to him—without irony—as "the King o' Sheep."

"Hmm," muttered Diggy, eyes narrowed. "If ye help Diggy find Bubs…"

"Of course, sir," replied Flynn gallantly. "The hounds'll lend their noses, won't they, lads?"

He gave a sharp whistle. The dogs bounded back through the reeds, tails thrashing, one of them proudly carrying the fallen pheasant in its jaws. The priest bagged the bird neatly, slung it behind him, and gestured to the old man.

"Come on then, your Majesty's Shepherd," he said. "Let's go find the king before the throne goes empty."

And so, the odd pair set off across the moor—one stooping, one wheezing, both talking at once—while behind them the lady of Stratford Hall turned toward home, smiling faintly at the absurd holiness of men.

THREE

After making his rounds through the factory—surveying the looms, the shipping bays, the storage halls, and the ledgers of margin with the Hedge brothers plodding dutifully beside him—Mr. Levi Jonathan Bairstow at last dismissed his attendants with a wave of imperial fatigue. He sauntered alone back to his tiny office, which, by design rather than chance, was situated directly beside the employees' entrance of the L. J. Bairstow Textiles Company. There, he might watch his workers come and go like penitents at a chapel gate.

Within that cramped sanctum stood a mahogany *secrétaire*, its drawers perpetually half-open and stuffed with curling papers, ledgers, and unpaid invoices. Beside it sat what the employees, with grim amusement, called "the Throne"—a ridiculous winged armchair of dark mahogany, upholstered in cracked burgundy leather. From this seat of mock majesty, Mr. Bairstow would preside, pen poised dramatically above parchment, glaring at every laborer who crossed the threshold, as though each one were a thief caught mid-theft. When an unfortunate soul met his eye, Bairstow would sigh heavily, as if disturbed in the midst of some grand mercantile calculation, and mutter, "Disgraceful," under his breath for good measure.

Upon this particular afternoon, however, it was Bairstow himself who became the startled subject of scrutiny. For when he turned the key and pushed open the door, he discovered a figure already seated in his chair—the seat of judgment now occupied by the judge himself.

"Mr. Hill!" cried Bairstow, his usual scowl rearranging itself into a grotesque parody of delight. "Well, bless me soul, to what do I owe the honor, sir?"

Mr. John Henry Hill of the Bank of England sat motionless, draped in an air of mourning. He was a tall, spare man, encased in a black suit of such funereal solemnity that one might mistake him for a walking hearse. His gloved hands rested neatly upon a polished walking stick, and a plume of white smoke from the ornate pipe in his mouth wreathed his face like a spectral halo.

"Another death, sir," he said, in a voice that carried neither shock nor sympathy—merely accountancy.

Bairstow drew himself up, his florid cheeks quivering. "Mr. Hill, I 'ave but this very hour inspected the floors myself—myself, sir!—and I'll have you know our premises are safer than the pews at St. Martin's!"

"Stoppage, sir," interrupted the banker without inflection. "There was stoppage."

"We 'ave never missed a shipment, nor a payment, nor a promise, and we shall not begin today," protested Bairstow, forcing a smile that wobbled like unset jelly. But within, his pulse was drumming.

"Are you quite in control, Mr. Bairstow?" Hill inquired, adjusting his spectacles. "The Bank is concerned. The town's reputation hangs by a thread. Complaints against manufacturers such as yourself reach London—letters from landowners, from Lord Dryden himself. The Bank of England does not merely desire profit; it desires stability."

Bairstow's expression darkened. "Lord Dryden and all 'is merry men are red wiff arrogance and green wiff envy! I built this factory wiff me bare 'ands! The very notion that a man of humble birth should outwit them in commerce turns their noble stomachs!"

Mr. Hill regarded him as one might a yapping terrier. "Sir, I have not come to hear your social philosophy. I am here to inquire after our investment, and to remind you of your responsibilities. There must be no further deaths, and no more grievances. Discontent, once whispered among the poor, spreads like cholera among the rich. That, sir, is *not good for business.*"

Bairstow puffed out his chest and placed a trembling hand over his waistcoat. "As I 'ave assured you, not a penny shall be lost! As for the unfortunate accident, I am exonerated—by law and by conscience! If another poor soul should perish upon this factory floor, I shall rest knowing I did everyfing—absolutely everyfing—within mortal power to prevent it. I am not God, Mr. Hill, nor can I prevent foolish children from their foolish childishness."

"Then pray, sir," said Hill, rising, "that it does not happen again."

He tapped the ash from his pipe against Bairstow's desk—once, twice, thrice—a hollow, deliberate sound—and replaced the pipe in his mouth.

Bairstow attempted one last simpering tone. "I trust, sir, you'll convey to your superiors my unshakable devotion to both profit *and* propriety?"

But Mr. Hill did not answer. He replaced his hat, nodded curtly, and walked out without another word.

For several moments after the door shut, Bairstow stood motionless, glowering at the smoke that lingered in the air. Then he sat slowly in his chair—the chair from which he had been so unceremoniously ousted—and muttered, "Another death, eh? Well then, the dead can't complain."

And with that, he reached for his pen, dipped it in ink, and began scratching figures upon the nearest ledger, as though to erase the living with arithmetic.

FOUR

The lifeless body of Tildon Allen lay bare upon the undertaker's table, pale and thin as paper, his limbs arranged with that mock dignity death affords the poor. The faint light from a single candle trembled against the damp walls, making the shadows of the instruments seem to crawl.

Dr. Horace Harland Blythe—physician, coroner, and self-professed man of science—stood over the body, pen and commonplace book in hand, scribbling with industrious zeal. From time to time he muttered to himself, nodding like one approving a well-performed lecture. He paused now, adjusted his spectacles, and gently turned Til's small head to one side, revealing a dark gash beneath the left ear. The doctor bent low, examining the wound with almost tender curiosity before resuming his furious note-taking.

"Poor little devil," sighed Mr. Perley Robert Wilbur, the undertaker, his thin falsetto trembling. "Poor, poor Til."

Wilbur's voice was naturally high and mournful, but on this occasion it had reached a pitch of exquisite lamentation. The sight of the penniless boy—an orphan with no one to finance his final voyage into the earth—had touched even Perley's long-calloused heart. He cast a glance toward the narrow coffin in the corner, the one Dr. Blythe had insisted he provide *gratis*, and sighed again, deeper still. "Poor, poor Til," he repeated, wringing his hands like a man trying to conjure sympathy from the air.

"Thank you, Perley," said Dr. Blythe without looking up. "That should suffice for—"

Boom! Boom!

The door at the end of the narrow passage shook under a heavy knock. Both men froze.

Blythe lifted his head, listening. Then, with the brisk calculation of a man who had left too many bodies behind in too many rooms, he said quietly, "I'll let myself out the back." He gathered his notebook, pressed his hat low over his brow, and slipped soundlessly through the mud-room door, vanishing into the fog beyond.

Perley Wilbur, left to face the interruption, picked up the flickering candle from beside the corpse. The flame cast grotesque shapes across his round, sweaty face as he shuffled sideways down the narrow hall. His considerable girth brushed every piece of furniture on the way; the buffet rattled, a stack of plates trembled, and the candle wax dripped like slow blood upon the floor. By the time he reached the end, he was panting so heavily that the knocking ceased of its own accord.

Drawing a deep breath, he heaved the iron bar from its latch and pulled open the door.

The cold night air rushed in, carrying with it two figures in blue greatcoats: Constable Hiram Walter Blackwood and his irrepressibly cheerful subordinate, Junior Constable Philip David Whitehouse.

"Good evening, Constables," Perley managed, voice quavering.

"Good evening, Mr. Wilbur," replied Constable Blackwood in his steady, martial tone. The man spoke as though every word were drilled upon parade ground.

"Merry Christmas, Perley!" cried Whitehouse with indecorous joy, raising his cap. "God bless this house!"

Constable Blackwood exhaled sharply through his nose, as if restraining the spirit of homicide. He continued, without looking at his partner, "Is Mr. William Avondale or Dr. Blythe here, perchance?"

"No, sir," said Perley quickly. "They've come and gone, for certain."

"It's an odd business, Mr. Wilbur," said Blackwood, his cold eyes narrowing. "Those two visiting after hours—and presumably the body. What precisely was their errand?"

"Mr. Avondale remarked," said Perley, attempting dignity, "that he was unable to attend poor Til's burial—the factory would not grant him leave—so I presume he came to pay his respects. As for Dr. Blythe, his interest in the boy was, ah, *scientific* in nature. He examined the body, took notes, and departed. Quite proper."

Whitehouse clapped his hands together with idiotic enthusiasm. "Fascinating—positively fascinating! What you gentlemen do for the town—positively *fascinating!* Good show, Perley, good show!"

Constable Blackwood closed his eyes briefly, as though counting to ten in Latin. Then, without a word, he pivoted toward the door. "I'm sure, Mr. Wilbur," he said at last, "that I shall see you at the pub this very evening."

With that, he stepped into the night, hands clasped neatly behind his back, marching with the same rigid precision that had once made him a terror to deserters.

Whitehouse lingered in the doorway, waving cheerfully at the undertaker. "Merry Christmas again, Mr. Wilbur! Give my regards to the dear departed!"

The younger constable laughed at his own jest and trotted after his superior, who by then was halfway down the misty lane toward *Ye Olde Knights of Jerusalem.*

Perley stood in the open doorway for a long moment, the candle flickering in his trembling hand. Then, with a shuddering breath, he turned back toward the silent room, where poor Til lay waiting—eyes closed, secrets sealed.

"Poor, poor Til," he murmured again, closing the door against the wind.

FIVE

At precisely the stroke of seven, snowflakes began to fall outside *Ye Olde Knights of Jerusalem*, and the men within burst into spontaneous cheer. Winter, long delayed and much desired, had finally come to England—three full weeks into December. The mild season had overstayed its welcome, and the town, festooned and waiting, had grown restless. Mrs. Woolly's crimson banners drooped from their hooks, the doors along Main Street stood crowned with wreaths commissioned by the town council, and shepherds and angels in plaster had been stationed about the green—awaiting a white backdrop that never came. Until tonight. When the first flakes fell past the gaslights, the townsmen raised their glasses to salute the turning of the heavens, as though the ancient gods themselves had relented to their prayers.

"Ale for the table, and plenty of it!" cried old Blanchard the brewer, as mugs clinked in every direction. The air thickened with smoke and laughter.

At the far end of the pub, seated in the dimmest corner near the hearth, Mr. John Henry Hill of the Bank of England took his supper in solitude. His only companion was his elderly attendant, Mr. Cowley, who stood a pace behind him, watching the festivities with disapproval so sharp it might have sliced the very mirth from the room. Cowley leaned on his cane, the top of which was carved into the shape of a lion's head. A long, pale scar bisected the right side of his face—from forehead to jawline—a souvenir, he often muttered, from a Frenchman who had failed to finish the job at Waterloo.

Hill ate mechanically, the clatter of forks and the bellow of laughter leaving no impression on him. His eyes flicked once toward the revelers, then back to his plate. Cowley's scowl deepened.

At that moment, a commanding voice rose above the din. Mayor Eldon Samuel Craig—red-faced and already rather soused—stood upon the bar like a conquering hero surveying his domain. He held his tankard high and bellowed, "Gentlemen, I propose three toasts!" The room fell obligingly quiet. "First, to the gentle dusting we receive this night—heaven's own benediction upon our Holy Days! Second, to the fine gentleman seated among us this evening, Mr. L. J. Bairstow—bringer of commerce, purveyor of textiles, benefactor of our humble town! And third, to the industrious poor, who even now drink down at the *Headless Horseman*—may their wages ever find their way to Main Street—into your pockets, gentlemen! To Levi Bairstow!"

"Levi Bairstow!" roared the crowd, mugs clashing like sabres.

Mr. L. J. Bairstow, seated by the great stone fireplace, rose slightly, raising his glass with a satisfied nod. His round face shone pink in the firelight, and his gold watch chain glimmered at his waistcoat. He was the kind of man who could accept adoration without surprise.

From the doorway came Constable Blackwood, his heavy boots leaving a trail of melted snow behind. He made for Bairstow's table with the grim expression of a man who had seen too much mirth for one evening, and sat down with a sigh. Behind him followed Constable Whitehouse—a far more cheerful specimen—who hummed *Deck the Halls* under his breath as though the entire evening were a holiday pageant.

"Constable Whitehouse," said Bairstow with a grin, sloshing his ale as he raised it, "you've the voice of an angel, and I've heard my share of choirs."

"I don't deserve to be so merry, sir," the young constable said, scratching the back of his neck, "not with little Tildon's death still under inquiry."

At once the room seemed to chill, the laughter dimming like a fire gone to ash.

Whitehouse went on, awkward but earnest. "And if I'm being plain, I ought to be disappointed in *you*, Mr. Bairstow—sending those boys up on the rafters after the warning you'd been given! William told me himself! A lad like Tildon ought never to have been made to climb. I wouldn't be surprised if a Royal Commission took an interest in the plight of the working poor before long." He hesitated, then added quickly, "Still—it's a week to Christmas Day, and I shan't let suspicion spoil good company."

Levi Bairstow laughed—too loudly, too long. "There's an honest man," he said to his associate Adoniram Hedge, "as honest as the night is dark! And there's another thing—there's a man who knows not a whit of how the world turns. By the sweat of a man's brow, that's how, and by the profits of those who dare employ him. You're free to your opinions, Constable, but you're not free to cast a cloud upon my affairs in a public house such as this!"

Whitehouse's smile stiffened, then fell away. He swallowed and said, "I'm an officer of the law, and I—"

"—can go to 'ell. I've had the law and the mayor inspect my fine facility, who boff sang praise as to the tenderness wiff which I and the Hedges shepherd the flock. Now sod off, runt." Levi's voice was silk that could scratch; the pub went quiet enough to hear the snow settling outside.

The unfortunate Whitehouse glanced at Blackwood for help. Blackwood, who had not moved a muscle through the exchange, kept his face a careful mask. Whitehouse shrugged, humiliated, and melted back into the crowd like a bad cough. He disappeared through the knot of bodies toward the door, shoulders hunched against the winter, his hymn-book tucked under his arm like a talisman that failed to charm.

Levi turned his glass by the handle, eyes narrowing. "Constable—how goeth thy errands?" he asked, throwing the question like a lasso.

Blackwood flinched at the quaintness of the phrasing—Levi's old-world taunt—and leaned in. The pub's warmth felt suddenly thin. He dropped his voice. "The Doctor and Avondale have not ceased their inquisition—they were at Perely's only this evening."

Levi's smile went hard. He scanned the room; Hill and Cowley who'd been in the corner were gone—no trace but the ash in their cups. Levi's glance snagged on Sam Hedge, who sat stiff as a post; his brothers, Adoniram and Sam's two hulking kin, edged forward until they loomed like thunderstorms.

"What thou must do, do thou quickly, my son," Levi said, almost tender. It was a command disguised as counsel.

Blackwood put a hand to Levi's forearm, meant to moderate. "Now Levi—"

The Hedge brothers leaned in together, a pair of beasts who had learned to read the world by the angle of a man's jaw. Blackwood's hand, like a man's in a room full of boiling pans, retreated to the safety of his beer. The movement cost him nothing, but it was noted.

Levi's voice dropped, the clipped consonants of his working-class accent flooding the public manner with a private cruelty. "I don't… give… a piss… what you 'fink… or want. I have been given the unpleasant task of 'erdin' these pathetic lil' sheep, and with that task comes the responsibility of killin' wolves, Constable Blackwood. You, sir, are paid to guard the interests of the town, and the interests of the factory are the interests of the town—on top of which you are paid, over and above, by myself."

The last clause was the fulcrum—the moment money turned law into suggestion. Around the table, men who had laughed a breath earlier now watched the tension like a stagehand watches a trapdoor.

"The Banks enforce their interests by the law, and I enforce my interests by my law—and that may or may not include you. Avondale must be taught a lesson. End of. Adoniram will 'ave a word with the Doctor, and if he decides to be a wolf, then he too shall be punished. But don't you ever lay hand on me again, Blackwood—else Sam 'ere think ye a wolf."

Blackwood's mouth opened and closed. He straightened, clutched his jacket as if to pull himself into proper posture, and for a second looked very young. "Apologies, Levi," he said, the starch in the apology thin and brittle. "I was only thinking it could be too soon to deal so—er, drastically with Avondale, seeing as Til—"

"Were you about to say Tildon? Don't you dare pin that on me!" Levi barked. The room drew in a collective breath; even the fireplace seemed to hold its flame, before Levi returned to a whisper. "That boy died of his own foolishness. And nobody's said anyfin about killin' Avondale. Never mind, never mind—I don't give a piss what you fink. You ain't paid to fink—you're paid to lean. I will decide what's drastic, and besides, Sam 'ere 'as ways of makin' fings look... natural. Bruises from the stairs, that sort of fing. No one will be the wiser. Now piss… off."

A laugh like water running through a half-closed tap leaked from someone at the end of the bench—nervous, quick—but the jeer had been swallowed by the room's new gravity. Blackwood rose, adjusted his jacket with hands that trembled very slightly, and made his way to the bar as if in a slow, obedient procession. He did not reach for his purse that night; it remained in his pocket, weightless and impotent.

Levi watched him go, the corner of his mouth curling with the satisfaction of a man who had trimmed the hedges without soiling his gloves. He leaned back toward Sam, voice low and honeyed. "Something must also be done about Whitehouse."

Sam Hedge's eyes glittered. "We'll take care of the songster," he said softly. "A warning, nothing more. Let him know the tune on his lips ought match the tune in his heart." He tapped the table with the flat of his hand, a private benediction.

Outside, the snow fell thicker, muffling footsteps and scandal alike. Inside *Olde Knights*, the lamps burned on, and men who had come for ale and a white winter left with a sterner knowledge of who kept the town's ledger—and who kept the town's silence. The nativity on the green would be dusted with the same snow that hid wrongs, for a while at least, under a clean and merciful white. But the work of unmaking that whiteness would begin in the morning—at the mills, the bank, the infirmary—and in the small, anxious rooms where constables and doctors met, words like "inquest" and "commission" tasted like icicles on the tongue.

Levi drained his mug, smiled as if to himself, and raised it once more to the faces around him. "To Main Street," he said. "And to what keeps Main Street running." The glasses went up. The men drank. The snow kept falling.

SIX

"She finks it's just too dangerous, Wiww," said Mr. James Bennet Wesley, stirring his ale with the contemplative air of a man expecting divine intervention to rise from its froth. "Too bloody dangerous, it is. And Bairstow don't give a shilling, neither. He'll just gather up more o' them orphaned lot—work 'em on the Mules till they've no fingers nor eyes left. Never mind the beams he's got the little rats scurryin' on in that storage loft. I seen one near fall just last week—caught his breeches on a nail and hung there like a Sunday ham."

William Avondale rubbed his temples, his drink untouched. "Who else do I talk to, Jim? I've done and said everythin' I could—I even went to Dr. Blythe himself. But what are men to do when even the Law's against 'em? I'll try to get Ann off the Jenny tomorrow, but I can't promise anything—the Hedges are everywhere, crackin' their sticks and scarin' the saints out of everyone…"

"I know you're one of us, Wiww," said Wesley, softening. "I know your best is bein' done."

From the corner of the table, a voice broke in—Mr. Merrill John Kidd, who always smelled faintly of cabbage and old ink. "What if we went to Lord Dryden?"

The barkeep, Mr. Henry Isaac Dosett, who had been polishing the same glass for ten minutes purely for the sake of eavesdropping, let out a scoff. "Oh come off it, Merrill. Lord Dryden's too busy countin' his portraits of himself."

"No, Henry," Jim said thoughtfully, eyes narrowing as if squinting at a far-off miracle, "it may be a worthy idea. Lord Dryden is a powerful man with powerful connections."

"Lord Dryden," Avondale began, "is a pompous, high-born, perfumed—"

Before he could finish, Henry seized Avondale's arm sharply. The door had opened with the chime of its cracked bell. Father Flynn had entered—his robes dusted with snow, his cheeks red from the cold—with Diggy trailing behind like a loyal yet hopelessly unwashed shadow.

"Evenin', Father. Diggy," said Henry quickly, summoning a grin that belonged more to a salesman than a saint. "What'll it be tonight, gentlemen?"

"Two pints of Guinness with whiskey chasers, Henry," said Flynn, shaking off the chill.

Henry, without missing a beat, smirked. "And for you, Diggy?"

The bar erupted. Tankards rattled, and Merrill John Kidd nearly spilled his pint.

"I can still knock the crown off a quid, Henry Dosett," replied Father Flynn, his brogue deep as a church bell. "Ya cheek. Sit down, Isaac, before I anoint you with yer own whiskey."

Laughter rolled again, and even Diggy—poor Diggy, with his matted hair, sheepish eyes, and smell of damp wool and misfortune—let out a shy chuckle. Flynn clapped him on the back and guided him to a stool at the bar. The regulars, despite their jokes, admired the priest's odd charity. Father Flynn had a habit of collecting strays—souls and otherwise—and bringing them where warmth could work its small miracles.

Diggy, with a fresh pint before him, sat taller than usual. There was something sacramental in it—this small act of inclusion. The room grew quieter, gentler.

"To Bubs, Gid!" Diggy said suddenly, lifting his glass high, his voice shaking with feeling.

The men, caught off guard but moved, echoed him. "To Bubs!" they said, and their mugs met with the sound of honest metal.

They drank.

A moment of stillness followed—no one spoke, but every man's eyes flicked toward the hearth where the snowlight flickered. Then Father Flynn rose a little in his seat and spoke softly, "Prayers will be offered up for the soul of young Tildon Allen at tomorrow's mass. I know a great many of ye'll be at labor, and so I shall offer up prayers for thy souls as well."

There were nods all around, and even Henry paused his polishing. For a heartbeat, the *Headless Horseman* ceased to be a pub and became, improbably, a parish.

Another moment of quiet passed as the men nursed the last of their ale. The fire crackled in the grate, sending tiny comets of ash up the chimney, and the only sound was the faint hiss of snow against the windowpanes. Father Flynn, wiping the foam from his mustache with the back of his sleeve, looked as though he might begin a sermon; but before he could, William Avondale leaned forward, his elbows on the sticky oak table.

"Father," he said, breaking the hush, "how would a man go about seeing Lord Dryden?"

Flynn raised a brow. "Stratford Hall is always open, William."

"Aye," said Avondale, shifting uneasily. "Open, perhaps—but Lord Dryden always seems... indisposed."

Flynn smiled faintly, the kind of smile that belonged to a man who had seen through many doors that were supposed to be locked. "Come Saturday for tea as me guest—he never misses Saturday tea."

Avondale straightened, his expression one of surprised gratitude. "I will, sir. I surely will."

And with that, William Avondale—floor master for L. J. Bairstow Textiles Co., husband to no one, father to none, and friend to few—finished what remained of his ale, settled his account at the *Horseman*, and rose to go. He bid his company goodnight, pulled his coat tight about him, and stepped into the white world beyond the door.

The night had grown deeper and quieter, the kind of quiet that presses on the eardrums like a held breath. The snow, thick and luminous under the gaslamps, fell in slow, ponderous flakes the size of sixpence coins. Avondale trudged up the narrow hill that split the town in two, his boots crunching through the brittle crust. To his left, the cheerful racket of *Olde Knights* rolled faintly through the wind—singing, shouting, the occasional crash of glass. The sound of life and drink. But on his side of the hill, the world was deathly still.

He passed St. George's Chapel, its pointed windows aglow with the faint light of a single taper inside, and the adjacent cemetery where rows of headstones stood like stoic sentries in the snow. The wind, mischievous and cruel, swept suddenly down from the ridge, catching the brim of his hat and plucking it neatly from his head.

"Blast!" he muttered, watching it tumble end over end, a dark blur against the white, until it landed near the old stable well—an ancient stone ring half-buried in drifts.

Avondale hurried after it, head down, the flakes stinging his face. He reached the well, where the hat had lodged in the snow along its rim. He bent over, one hand on the icy stone, the other reaching for the hat's brim.

At that instant, there came a sound—a footstep, soft but certain—then a tremendous shove between his shoulder blades.

Avondale lurched forward, his cry cutting the stillness. His hands clawed at the rim, scraped ice, found nothing. His body vanished into the black mouth of the well, swallowed whole, his voice echoing briefly before it was silenced by a sickening crack as his skull met a jutting stone twelve feet below. Then came the splash—deep, final, and absolute.

Above, the wind howled over the rooftops and the chapel spire. The hat, that wretched truant, sat perfectly still on the snow, its brim catching flakes until it was white again—as though nothing at all had happened.

SEVEN

The pub had finally emptied out—the hour half past two—and Henry Dosett was alone with the dying fire. The laughter and boots and bawdy songs of the night had faded into memory, leaving only the whisper of the wind against the windowpanes and the occasional settling groan of the timbered roof. The last mug was polished, the floor swept, the coins counted and tucked into the till. Henry placed the final tankard on the high shelf, exhaled, and stretched his back.

He crossed the room to the hearth, poker in hand, and stirred the embers, watching sparks leap and vanish like startled souls. The fire had shrunk to a red, crawling undergrowth, pulsing faintly in the shadows. He muttered something to himself about turning in. The door was bolted; the lamps dimmed. He had the strange satisfaction of solitude—the kind that turns sour if it lingers too long.

Then came the sound.

It was not a gust of wind but something stranger—the wind drawn *inward*, as though the air itself were being swallowed. The shutters rattled, the flame bent backward toward the chimney, and the hairs along Henry's arms lifted like soldiers at attention. The sound grew—a howl, then a shriek, then something between the two—and from it came a voice that did not belong to the living.

"Hhhhhhhhhhhhhhhhenry."

The syllables slid like frost down the back of his neck.

He spun around, poker raised.

The door had unlatched itself. The air shimmered, blue and cold and wavering like gaslight over water. From that phosphorescent fog, a figure began to form—first a blur, then a man—dressed as he had been in life, with a dark, wet gash running down the left side of his head.

Henry's mouth went dry. "William?—What the blue hell are you?"

The apparition tilted its head, its eyes pale and steady. When it spoke, its voice came in layers—one deep, one high, one echoing through the walls.

"I wasssssss… and I willllll beeeeeee… yet I ammmmm not yyyyyetttt."

"Oh God help me," Henry whimpered.

Avondale drifted forward, his boots hovering an inch above the floorboards. Henry stepped back, his heel knocking against a chair. He braced himself, lifting the poker like a cricketer facing a ghostly bowler.

"Looooook, Hhhhhhhhhenryyyyyy," came the moan.

The specter bowed its head, revealing the wound—wide, glistening, the skin pale around it like marble. Bloodless, but freshly made.

Henry swung in terror, the iron cutting straight through the ghost with a hiss, scattering the embers and sending him sprawling into a table. The poker clanged on the floor. The ghost did not move, only hung there, still bent, its hand raised in pitiful invitation.

Henry crawled backward, his breath short and shallow. "Okay, William. What are we lookin' at, old friend?"

"Looooook what theyyyyy've donnnnnne," whispered the ghost. Its voice trembled the glassware.

Henry's eyes followed the translucent hand to the ruin on the left temple—the crushed bone, the dent where the skull had split.

"Who, Will? Who done this?"

"I knowwwwwweth not, Hhhhhhenryyyyy. Hhhhhhhhelp meeeee."

And then the air shifted again—the ghost's edges pulling inward as though yanked by invisible ropes. The wind reversed itself once more, howling back through the doorway, dragging the specter with it. The last of Avondale's face dissolved in a streak of blue light that fled into the night.

The fire guttered, the beams groaned, the candles surrendered one by one.

Henry stood frozen, hands shaking at his mouth, eyes wide as the dark closed in. When the final ember blinked out, silence fell so completely that he could hear his own pulse pounding like a drum in a coffin.

And in that silence, Henry Dosett—the practical man, the unbelieving barkeep, the scoffer of sermons—felt a spreading warmth down his leg. It ran slow and steady into his boot, seeping through wool and leather alike, until the pub was as still as the grave and he was left trembling in it, praying that morning would quickly come.

EIGHT

The body of William Avondale was discovered just after dawn by Mrs. Adeline Mary Mulford—widow of the late Mr. G. A. Mulford, Cooper—whose own husband had met an ignoble end some years prior at the Werely County Ladies' Archery Invitational, where a misfired arrow (from a Mrs. Priscilla Bunting, no less) had lodged most inconveniently in his thorax. Since that day, the widow Mulford had been known throughout town for her strict adherence to order, cleanliness, and the fear of God, all three of which she considered interchangeable.

She had risen early, as was her custom, to fetch eggs from her hens, those anxious creatures she doted upon with both affection and tyranny. As she crossed the yard, her sharp eyes fell upon the churchyard beyond her fence—the ground adjoining St. George's Chapel—and she froze. The pail, her dear husband's handiwork, was gone again, vanished into the black throat of the old well.

Now, few things vexed Mrs. Mulford more than negligence—especially negligence committed at the *hallowed springs of St. George*. In her estimation, this was not mere thoughtlessness, nor even sacrilege, but "a total disregard for the sanctity of the Church of England," and—what was worse—a personal insult to the eternal repose of the parish dead. Setting her basket of eggs aside (where they promptly rolled into the mud and cracked), she marched across the frost-hardened path, skirts snapping in the wind, to the well. She seized the rope with both hands and yanked it, muttering a string of condemnations that would have blistered a curate's ears. The line would not move.

"Stubborn devil," she hissed, and pulled again, harder, until the veins stood out on her neck like cords. The windlass refused to budge.

Off she stormed—her eyes bright with outrage, her lips moving in silent recriminations—into the cottage, past the broken eggs, to prepare herself for war. She donned her late husband's steel-capped boots, then her thickest wool wrapper, and finally crowned herself with a straw bonnet tied severely over her mourning kerchief. Thus armoured, she summoned reinforcements: Mr. Thomas Mark Cummings, the Saddler; Mr. John David Pound, the Blacksmith; and Mr. Cecil Silas Switch, the Cobbler—all respectable tradesmen and equally terrified of her.

Together they tramped to the churchyard, the widow leading like a general on campaign. At her command, the men removed the little timbered roof that shaded the well, exposing the darkness within. They leaned over the stone rim—four curious faces peering into the cold.

It was Mr. Cummings who saw it first: a pale shape swaying beneath the surface, blue as skimmed milk.

"Jesus, Mary, and Joseph," he whispered.

"How'll we get *it* out?" asked Mr. Pound.

"He, Mr. Pound," the widow snapped, "the *deceased* has not stopped being a *person*." She looked more scandalized by the man's grammar than by the corpse itself.

"Constable Blackwood must be summoned at once," said Cummings, nervously rubbing his hands.

"Are you suggestin' it's murder, Thom?" asked the Cobbler.

"I'm suggestin' we allow Constable Blackwood to do *his job,* sir."

"Well, in the meantime," said Pound, "we can figure how to fetch the poor fellow out."

"An excellent notion, Mr. Cummings," said Mrs. Mulford (she had given Pound up as irredeemable), "and while we're at it, we must also assess the damage done to the well itself and the cost of restoration."

Pound and Switch exchanged a look of long-suffering and rolled their eyes skyward. But orders were orders, and they followed the widow uphill toward Blackwood's lodgings.

By the time Constable Blackwood had been roused, dressed, and fortified with a cup of Mrs. Aldershot's strong breakfast tea, word of the discovery had already flown through the town like gossip on a gale. When he reached St. George's, a crowd had gathered—wives, children, factory hands on break—all craning for a look. The good people of Werely, eager to help, had trampled the ground so thoroughly that any useful trace was ground into the mud.

Blackwood cursed under his breath and waved the onlookers back. "Right then," he said. "Let's see him up."

The men of the town set to work. A noose was fashioned and dropped around the protruding foot, and with the help of Mr. Philip Eli Winter—who produced a retired gaff from his fishing days—the corpse was hauled from the depths "in two shakes of a lamb's tail," as Pound cheerfully observed, earning a withering glare from the widow.

When the sodden form hit the grass, there was no mistaking him: William Avondale, floor master of L. J. Bairstow Textiles.

His face was contorted, his coat stiff with frost, his hair matted to his ruined temple.

"Best get him to Wilbur's," said Blackwood grimly.

So it was done. The body was carried to the undertaking rooms of Mr. Perley Robert Wilbur—whose enthusiasm for his trade rarely survived the financial aspect of it—and placed upon the table. Dr. Horace Harland Blythe soon arrived, spectacles glinting, notebook in hand.

Wilbur grumbled about the "donation" of another coffin, Dr. Blythe began his examination with brisk detachment, and Constable Blackwood, weary and hungry, accepted a luncheon offered by several well-meaning busybodies.

And while the townsfolk whispered outside, Mrs. Mulford stood in the doorway, arms crossed, watching the men of science and law do their work. She was still muttering about the desecration of holy ground—but under her breath now—because for all her talk of sanctity, she could not quite shake the feeling that something else, something unholy, had been stirred in the well that morning.

NINE

Lord Dryden crumpled the letter with a sharp twist of his wrist, the paper crackling like a musket misfire. He clasped his hands behind his back, drawing a long, deliberate breath to steady himself—but composure was a fickle ally. With sudden fury, he swung his leg and kicked the couch. The spaniels leapt up in alarm, barking their outrage.

"Apologies, lads!" he barked, though the apology rang hollow.

"Apologies, nothin'," said Father Flynn, stern as a confessor. "Ye have cause to be angry, Lord!"

"Forgive me, Cat—"

"Never mind, Father—it's horrible, and something *ought* to be done!" said Catherine, her eyes flashing as she coolly lifted Flynn's rook and replaced it with her bishop. The priest winced, seeing his checkmate vanish under the guise of moral fervor.

"I am simply astonished," said Dryden, resuming his pacing, "at the unwillingness of the law even to *review* the practices of the mill! Of course, I should be accused of hypocrisy for showing compassion, since I have land of my own—heaven forbid a gentleman care for those beneath him! Or worse still, they'd say I meddle for profit—'unfair economics,' I believe the phrase is."

He strode back and forth across the Persian rug, the dogs trotting anxiously in his wake. "Perhaps they like what the mills have done to Manchester, but I do *not!* It was only last year I rode through those streets—God save me, I thought I'd stumbled upon another battlefield. Half the people were missing limbs! The stench of sickness, the gray faces—it was Waterloo all over again."

He stopped, lowering his voice. "One of my companions told me of a boy—caught by the strap of a machine. Poor devil had just woken from sleep. They found him in *pieces.*"

The words hung in the air like smoke.

Father Flynn closed his eyes. Catherine set down her bishop.

Dryden swallowed, hearing again the echo of his mother's voice: *'Mind your tongue before the girl, George. Spare her the officers' club talk.'*

He turned to Catherine, softened. "Forgive me, Cat—"

"Dear Jesus," Father Flynn gasped as he held a hand to his stomach, looking queasier by the moment. "I think I'll have a bit of whiskey, to help the stomach…"

"You will not!" Catherine berated. "For we have an appointment in the yard, remember?" She winked at the priest, who looked confused and began to protest:

"But it's freezin' and—," Flynn stopped mid sentence, suddenly remembering what Catherine was hinting at. "—and the dogs may as well have a dash in the snow, stretch 'ter legs," he neatly finished, gesturing to the hounds, who had long given up any hope of receiving scraps and had instead retired back to their usual spot by the fire.

"Charles," Lord Dryden called, "have my carriage readied—I'm going into town."

"Lord."

"Erm—Lord…leave yer sword at home," Flynn joked.

"I'm going to pay an amicable visit to *Ye Olde—*"

Flynn smiled and held Dryden's gaze.

"Many of the men served under me, Flynn, don't look at me like that."

Flynn didn't move.

"I'm staying away from that insufferable opportunist."

"Never 'tot otherwise, Lord."

"What will you do, Catherine?"

"I'll accompany Father Flynn around the back with the dogs—"

"It's terribly cold out there, Cat—"

"I'll be fine, father."

"Flynn, if she catches her death I'm holding you personally responsible."

"Yes, Lord—and I shall see you later, perhaps—in town."

"Perhaps."

TEN

THWACK! went the flick against the wall—sharp, wet, and violent—as Sam Hedge loomed over a small, shoeless boy crouched beside a pile of lint and gears, wolfing down a crust of bread. The boy froze, crumbs tumbling from his mouth, then leapt upright, trembling like a rabbit in a trap.

"Lunch is over, Billy boy, my love!" Sam bellowed, his voice all bile and mockery. He swung the leather flick again and again against the wall for emphasis, the sound echoing through the mill's stone belly. "Get to the side o' that mule before I show ye what for!"

Billy darted off, scrambling around the massive mechanized loom. His bare feet slapped the boards, leaving prints in the dust. He appeared on the far side just as Ms. Jane May Smith bent over the engine, her dark hair tied back with a red ribbon now gray with cotton.

"There's a good lad, Biw—don't you pay him no mind, miserable toss," Jane whispered, eyes still on the whirring machine as she adjusted a gear.

With a groan and a belch of steam, the loom came to life, belts spinning, iron rods clanking. A hanging bit of Jane's loose sleeve caught the turning wheel and pulled taut. She yelped, jerking her arm back as the fabric tore with a sound like ripping flesh.

"Damn thing!" she hissed, clutching the ragged edge of her sleeve.

"Roll 'em higher, Janie," Billy said earnestly, his voice small but sure. "They'll catch every time."

Jane glanced down at him and managed a quick smile—the kind of smile that could still survive in a place where everything else seemed designed to crush it.

Billy adored her. To him, Jane May Smith was more than a co-worker—she was warmth in a world of cold steel and colder men. Though she was only nineteen—ten years his senior—she had a mother's tenderness. She brought him scraps of food from home, tucked bits of bread in his hand, called him *love* when everyone else called him *rat.*

The Hedges, of course, had already taught him every vice worth knowing. Billy drank, swore, and hustled like a grown man. When the day's work was done, he and the other mill lads took their wages—or what was left of them—down to the *Headless Horseman.* On the bitterest nights, Henry Dosett let them sleep near the stove, curled up in sacks like stray dogs.

Billy and his late friend, Tildon Allen, had earned themselves a reputation in town—"Bairstow's Privateers," the men called them. The little devils made sport of haunting *Ye Olde Knights of Jerusalem*, eavesdropping on the merchants' boasts and then threatening to tell their wives precisely when they'd arrived and how much they'd spent. Their audacity usually bought them a few pennies to keep quiet.

By nightfall, the Privateers would swagger into the Horseman, pockets jingling, ordering mugs of ale with the solemnity of men twice their age. Henry Dossett, half amused and half heartbroken, would shake his head as the boys counted out their coins, wide-eyed and red-cheeked, drunk not only on ale—but on the dangerous thrill of being men before their time.

"Where did you sleep last night, love?" Jane asked softly, her voice half lost beneath the clatter of the looms.

Billy, rubbing his tired eyes with a grease-stained sleeve, replied, "Stayed 'ere, miss. No luck at the *'orseman*."

"Sam let you stay 'ere?" she said, frowning.

"Yeh—said I could stay a week if I keep me 'filffy mouff shut' and stay away from William."

Jane stopped her work and turned sharply toward him. "Shut yer mouth about *what*, Billy?"

The boy hesitated, lowering his head. "'Bout Til," he muttered. "William's been tellin' me not to go up on them planks no more—says it's too dangerous till it's fixed—and told me to tell the other Privateers."

Jane's face paled. "He did, did he? Well, you best stay away from William then, lad. Sam'll do a lot more than chase you round with flick if he hears otherwise. The factory's full of his spies, Biw—best keep your head down."

Before Billy could answer, a roar came from the far side of the mule. "Oi!" shouted Sam Hedge, his voice cracking like a whip. "What's with all the chitty-chitty chat-chat? Have I not made meself clear, Billy boy? Come 'ere, lil rat!"

Jane straightened, calling back, "Leave 'im alone, Sam—he was just tellin' me where more yarn is."

Sam's face reddened at being contradicted. "I weren't talkin' to *you*, Ms. Smiff," he spat, his words thick with malice. "'Ere, rat—get over 'ere!"

Billy shuffled forward, head down, his small hands trembling as he stretched them out before him. Sam met Jane's eyes, a cruel grin spreading across his face as he raised the leather strap high.

"This—" *whack!* "—is for that tongue o' yours, Biww." Another crack split the air, louder this time. "And this—" *whack!*"—is for that tongue o' yours, Ms. Smith."

The sound echoed through the rows of machines, mingling with the hum of belts and the hiss of steam. Jane bit into her sleeve to muffle her scream, the taste of oil and cotton dust filling her mouth as tears welled in her eyes.

Sam, satisfied, stepped back and smirked. "As you were, my loves. As you were." He gave Billy a shove toward Jane and swaggered off down the aisle, cracking the flick against his palm as he went, still barking orders to invisible sinners.

Billy stumbled back, blowing on his hands, where bright red welts had already begun to bloom across the skin. Jane caught him, pulled him close, and pressed a quick kiss to his forehead. Then, with trembling gentleness, she lifted his hands and kissed them too.

"There now," she whispered, voice breaking. "He won't always win, love. Not forever."

Wiping her tears with her torn sleeve, Jane strode to the front of the mule and slammed the brake bar forward. The machine wheezed to a halt. She tore the cloth free from its frame, muttering curses under her breath that would have startled a vicar, and set back to work—her movements furious, defiant, and very nearly holy.

ELEVEN

Catherine had fired the last musket ball into the line of wooden targets, each one scarred and splintered from her earlier enthusiasm. Her fingertips ached from the cold; even the musket's iron felt like ice against her gloves. She blew into her hands, slung the weapon over her shoulder, and turned toward the great house, whose chimneys puffed gray ribbons of smoke into the pale December air.

From across the snowy garden came the unmistakable voice of Father Flynn, booming like a cheerful cannon. "A warm cup o' tea—to be held by the hands—awaits us, young lady!"

Catherine laughed as she trudged up the path. "And I'm sure a warm cup of tea—to be mixed with a spirit—awaits *you*, Father Flynn."

"Aye, lass," he called back with mock solemnity. "The spirits is good for the spirits."

"Ha ha!" she said, shaking her head. "And I've found pound cake to be good for the spirit as well."

He raised his hands as if invoking the heavens. "A warm pound cake—fresh from the oven!"

She joined in the play, lifting her voice with theatrical grandeur. "A *Christmas* pound cake—warm from the oven—shared with friends and enemies alike!"

Father Flynn drew himself up, rolling his r's like a general announcing victory. "A *Chrrrrrristmas* pound cake—warm, frrrrrom the oven—shared with fffffrrrrriends and enemies alike, tea chaser, and a *checkmate delivered!*"

Catherine burst into laughter. "Oh yes, Father, I know that feeling well. When's the last time you actually *won* a game?"

"Catherine Dryden," he said, puffing out his chest in mock outrage, "I've taught you Latin, Greek, French, Arithmetic, Philosophy, Economics, Religion, Weaponry, and a great many other useless things—but the chess lessons—" he wagged a mittened finger—"*t'ain't nearly done!*"

Catherine grinned and quickened her pace toward the house, her breath rising in clouds, her cheeks red with cold and laughter. The great door swung open, spilling golden light and the smell of butter and tea into the snowy air.

Father Flynn was, to Catherine, an enduring mystery—a man of contradictions wrapped in cassock and laughter. He had soldiered in his youth, earning a scar across his temple in Spain, and later collected doctorates from Trinity as though they were souvenirs. Yet here he was, content to serve as tutor to the daughter of a famously disagreeable Anglican lord. It was a curious appointment, for Flynn had been a Catholic priest, and Lord Dryden was as staunch a Protestant as ever scowled at Rome.

And yet, somehow, they loved each other. Their friendship was a thing of paradox and wit—always an argument, never a quarrel. Flynn had taken the small parish of St. Mary's the very year before Catherine's birth, and when Lady Dryden's labor turned mortal, it was Flynn who had been called to her side. He had administered the last rites over her trembling hands, murmuring the Latin prayers of her childhood. She had begged her husband, between fading breaths, that the child be raised Catholic.

Lord Dryden, caught between pride and grief, agreed—grudgingly, stubbornly—but he kept his word. Every tutor thereafter was driven from Stratford Hall within a month by Dryden's impossible temper. Flynn alone endured, for no man could out-argue him, and no lord could truly despise him.

Dryden's in-laws, genteel and appalled, declared that the child was being "raised by two brutes"—a soldier and a heretic. Nevertheless, Catherine grew into a bright and steady girl, her winters spent under Flynn's eccentric instruction and her summers in Bath with her mother's family, who refined her into what they called *a proper young lady.*

Now, shaking the snow from her boots at the back door of Stratford Hall, she put on a mock-grave expression and announced in her best theatrical voice, "Very well, sir—thy student patiently awaiteth instruction."

Charles, the butler—tall, balding, and as solemn as a tomb—opened the door with his usual ceremony. He frowned deeply as the two pointers bounded past him, their paws printing muddy hieroglyphs across the marble floor.

"Forgive them, Charles," Flynn said cheerfully, stomping the snow from his own boots. "They're evangelists—they leave their mark everywhere."

Hats, gloves, coats, and boots were surrendered to the waiting servants and hung by the hearth to dry. The dogs were captured and toweled off, though they resisted with saintly enthusiasm. Catherine, cheeks flushed from the cold, followed Father Flynn into the parlor, where a generous fire danced beneath the marble mantel.

Tea arrived in fine porcelain, accompanied by pound cake still steaming from the oven. As they thawed, the room filled with the perfume of bergamot and butter and the sound of their laughter—an old priest and a young lady, defying propriety, faith, and the English winter in equal measure.

After they had sipped their tea for a while—Catherine delicately, Father Flynn noisily—the conversation settled into that comfortable quiet peculiar to winter afternoons. The fire popped, the wind breathed faintly against the windows, and the dogs lay curled before the hearth, twitching in their sleep. Catherine stirred her cup absently, then looked up from the steam.

"Why does Father so dislike that Bairstow fellow?" she asked at last.

Flynn gave a low hum, a sound between a sigh and a prayer. He stared into the fire for a moment, as if searching for the right words somewhere among the embers. "Ah, that is a question that reaches beyond dislike, my dear Cat. Your father has known all manner of rogues and politicians, but Bairstow—he offends something deeper."

He leaned back, his broad hands cradling the teacup with unusual gentleness. "When Diggy was sick last year, your father not only sent Mrs. Appleby with food and Dr. Blythe with medicine, but visited the poor man himself. I 'tink it was the visit of Lord Dryden that cured him. He sat by the bed and read aloud from *Pilgrim's Progress*, if you can believe it. And when Mrs. Adams lost her baby, he sent condolences to the husband—and then went himself. Took Adams to *Ye Olde Knights of Jerusalem*—can you imagine Adams in *Ye Olde*? The looks, Cat! The silence when they walked in. And there they sat, your father and the poor man, sharing ale and grief like equals. By the time they left, Adams had his laughter back. That's your father's way."

Catherine smiled faintly. "He pretends to be harsh, but he has a kind heart."

"Aye," said Flynn. "He does. He learned from his own father that the estate is more than a pile of acres and ledgers—it's a covenant. The people keep Stratford, and Stratford keeps them. It's not charity, exactly—it's kinship, though he'd never use so sentimental a word."

He shifted in his chair, the warmth of the fire glinting off his spectacles. "But this Bairstow fellow—he belongs to another age entirely. There's a new breed of men rising, Cat. Men who see laborers not as neighbors but as fuel. The old estate was a sort of purgatory—you toiled, yes, but you belonged somewhere. The factory…" He hesitated, the corner of his mouth tightening. "The factory is a place of judgment. No rest, no mercy, no humanity in it."

Catherine listened intently, her tea forgotten.

"Your father sees it clearly," Flynn went on. "Complaints are being made against mills like Bairstow's all over England. Withheld wages, mangled hands, children crushed by machines, women fainting from hunger and heat. Men like him call it progress. Your father calls it what it is—cruelty dressed as commerce."

He looked at her now, his expression soft but grave. "That's why your father despises him, Cat. Not for his success, but for the world he's building—the one that leaves no room for souls."

The fire popped again, and the silence returned, heavy and thoughtful.

"Why don't the men of the town do anything about it?" Catherine asked, setting her cup down with a clink. "And if this cruelty is happening all over England, why not Parliament—or the House of Lords?"

Father Flynn sighed, long and low, the kind of sigh that held both weariness and wisdom. "Ah, Cat, the men of Parliament are as tangled in their own strings as the spinners in Bairstow's mills. Lords like your father *have* been registering complaints—but it's a delicate business. The old landed families consider these matters beneath them. They think it poor form—vulgar, even—to be meddling in the affairs of what they call *trade*. The Bank, of course, encourages that notion."

He leaned forward, elbows on his knees, and spoke with a quiet intensity. "You see, the Banks don't stand to profit from your father. They profit from the upstarts—the Bairstowes of England. Cruel men who build new empires on broken backs. The Banks call it enterprise, but it's nothing more than legalized greed. So, Parliament and the Commons—whose careers depend on those very Banks—look the other way. They can't afford to see the truth, even when it bleeds before them."

Catherine's brow furrowed. "And the townsmen? Surely they must see the injustice?"

"They see it well enough," Flynn replied, "but they've been taught to call it order. What little wages the poor earn at Bairstow's mill go straight into the merchants' tills. The shopkeepers are fat, the constables content, and the clergy—well, the less said about the clergy in town, the better." His tone darkened. "They call it peace, but it's the peace of the graveyard."

He paused, swirling his tea absently. "And to make matters worse, there have been strange deaths—even here in Stratford."

Catherine straightened. "Surely *murder* is out of order! Shan't Colonel Blackwood look into it?"

Flynn barked a laugh, sharp and humorless. "Colonel Blackwood! More like Colonel *Blockhead.* The man's dense as an iron post and twice as heavy. He's become little more than Bairstow's errand boy—and the merchants' besides. And the merchants," he added with a crooked smile, "well, they're just the errand boys of the Bank."

"Then shall there be no justice for the poor?" she asked, her voice breaking slightly.

"There shall, Cat," Flynn said softly. "Lord Dryden will see to that. The Yard is not corrupt—*will not* be corrupt while he has breath. And I've spoken with William Avondale, one of the overseers at Bairstow's mill. He wishes to meet your father—to speak frankly about the conditions there. He's a brave man, that one. I believe he'll have much to say that the men of influence would do well to hear."

Catherine's eyes brightened, though her expression was grave. "What a gift that would be for the poor this Christmas," she said, her voice quiet as falling snow. "That their burden might at last be lightened."

TWELVE

The day had softened into that gray hour between afternoon and evening when the snow outside the windows glowed faintly blue and the world seemed to hush. Catherine sat before her vanity, still flushed from the cold and the thrill of target practice. Her musket lay propped against the corner wall—its gleam half hidden by her shawl, as though even the gun had been shamed into modesty within a lady's chamber.

She was brushing out her hair when Mrs. Havers entered without knocking, as was her ancient right. Havers had been in service since Lord Dryden's own christening, and she moved through Stratford Hall as one of its fixtures—steady, unstartled, practical as a clock.

"Ah, there ye are," she said, laying a folded linen over the arm of a chair. "Father Flynn says yer aim's improved. I told him it's the men's nerves, not yer marksmanship, that's slippin'."

Catherine smiled faintly. "You approve of my scandalous hobbies, then?"

Havers sniffed. "Hobbies keep a woman sane. You'd do better wi' a pistol than a needle, I should think. One punctures cloth, the other pretensions."

Catherine laughed, then fell quiet, gazing at her reflection in the mirror. "Do you think I ought to go to London, Havers?" she asked after a moment. "Father says it's time I rejoined 'the world.' My aunts in Bath write of balls and soirees as if they were matters of national importance. And yet..." She trailed off, still watching herself—the steady brown eyes, the high color from the cold, the faint smudge of powder on her sleeve. "When I imagine it—the drawing rooms, the gossip, the endless talk of lace and husbands—I feel as though I've been offered a part in a play I don't understand."

Havers gave a low chuckle and eased herself into a chair by the fire. "Yer not like other ladies, Miss Cat. Yer were raised by wolves."

Catherine turned from the mirror. "Wolves?"

"Aye," said Havers, nodding sagely. "Yer father an' Father Flynn. One growls, t'other howls. Between the two of 'em, they've taught ye more about piracy and politics than any finishin' school'd dare. Ye've the best o' both worlds, love—the masculine taste fer blood and the feminine serpentine subtlety to dance through a room full o' predators. Don't mistake that fer a fault. It's rare, that is."

Catherine rested her chin in her palm, half smiling, half frowning. "I sometimes worry it's made me... untethered. I'm not quite woman enough for London, and not quite savage enough for Stratford."

Havers looked at her over clasped hands. "That's the curse o' seein' too much, love. Ye can't go back to embroidery after ye've smelt gunpowder. Ye've seen what men are—what they'll do to keep their names an' lands. Ye've seen blood on snow an' called it beautiful. That doesn't make ye less of a woman. It makes ye honest."

Catherine studied the older woman. "You sound as though you've lived both sides yourself."

Havers gave a throaty chuckle. "Every woman has. The world just teaches us to hide it better. We smile an' curtsy, but inside we're keepin' count o' the men who think we don't see through 'em."

Outside, the wind rattled the windowpane, and the fire gave a low hiss.

The maid's face softened. "Stay close to yer father, lass. There's a shadow hangin' o'er this house. I feel it in me bones—like the smell before a storm. Evil's about, an' men like yer father an' Father Flynn'll be the first to stand against it. Ye'll need all yer wits—and that wolf's blood o' yours."

Catherine turned toward the window. The snow had begun again, soft and steady. "If evil is about," she murmured, "then I suppose I was raised for it."

"Aye," said Havers, rising slowly, her joints creaking like old oak. "An' heaven help the devil when he meets ye, Miss Cat."

Catherine smiled at her reflection again, half girl, half soldier, and whispered to herself, "Heaven help us both."

THIRTEEN

Constable Whitehouse had been given the unhappy task by Constable Blackwood: to deliver the news of William Avondale's death to his widow, Mrs. Abigail Ruth Avondale. It was, in every sense, a dreary duty, and Whitehouse—being of a sentimental nature—felt it deeply. The Avondales lived on a small, windswept parcel of land rented from Mayor Craig, who owned a collection of humble cottages on the edge of town. Their home was a short walk beyond the chapel, marked by a crooked chimney and a patch of bare garden that, in summer, sprouted more weeds than flowers.

Before setting off, Whitehouse thought to bring a peace offering. "Bad news travels lighter with bread," he muttered, and so he sent young Jimmy Houston, a local errand boy of dubious reliability, to fetch a loaf from the baker—one for the widow, and a roll for his own lunch. But as the quarter-hour passed and no Jimmy returned, Whitehouse began to suspect that charity and common sense were again at odds.

Muttering about the unreliability of youth, he marched himself to the bakery. The bell jingled as he entered, and Mrs. Sarah Bellingham looked up from her counter.

"Good day, Mrs. Bellingham. Has a boy come by for a loaf and a roll on my account?"

"Nobody's come in here, Constable Whitehouse—not for thirty minutes," she said, dusting flour from her hands.

Whitehouse frowned. "That little thief! Would you happen to know where one might find young Jimmy Houston at this hour, Mrs. Bellingham?"

She smiled knowingly. "If he isn't outside *Ye Olde Knights of Jerusalem* begging for pennies, he'll be at the Horseman drinking."

"That little thief!" Whitehouse repeated, this time with more wounded surprise than anger. "Good afternoon, madam."

And out he went, determined to catch the boy in the act. He strode down the cobblestone lane, his boots slipping slightly on the half-frozen slush. The air was heavy with the smell of coal smoke and horses. Turning down the narrow alley that ran between *Ye Olde* and the Bank, he spotted movement near a carriage. There, sure enough, was Jimmy Houston and two other little rascals, tugging a metal bar out of a gentleman's hitch.

The Privateers again.

It was one of their favorite tricks. When a "tight-fisted gentleman" refused to pay what the boys called the "Pirate Tax," they would loosen the carriage coupling, leaving the horse and reins to separate from the carriage the moment it moved. Only a week before, poor Mr. Eliot Jay Dimwhitty had suffered the consequences—his horse bolting up the street while he dove headfirst into a pile of manure, breaking his arm and his dignity at once.

"HEY! YOU THERE!"

The boys froze for a heartbeat, eyes wide—then scattered. Whitehouse gave chase.

Through the alley, up the narrow lane, and back down another alley they darted, laughing and shouting as the constable's heavy boots pounded behind them. His breath puffed white in the cold air; his coat flapped like a flag of war. The chase turned through a T-shaped passage between the warehouse and the pub's back wall. He stopped there, panting, looking left, then right. Empty.

"Over here, ya bloomin' codge!" one of the boys taunted, his voice echoing from nowhere. Giggles followed—high, cruel, mocking.

Whitehouse sighed, half smiling despite himself. "You devils…" he muttered, adjusting his cap. Then he remembered the parcel in his arm—the bread for poor Mrs. Avondale. Duty reclaimed him. He turned back toward the street.

And that was when it happened.

Something brushed against his chin, like a spider's thread. He reached up instinctively—but before he could swat it away, the thread pulled tight, biting into his throat. He tried to shout, but the sound strangled itself halfway out.

The wire jerked upward.

Whitehouse's boots left the ground. His back slammed against the wall of the *Horseman*. His eyes bulged with shock and disbelief as he clawed at the wire cutting into his neck. He kicked, scraping his heels against the brickwork, but the noose only tightened, rising higher, crushing his windpipe with a soft, deliberate creak.

The bread fell from his hands, landing softly in the snow.

No one heard him. No one saw. The street beyond was empty, the town already shuttered against the cold.

A few moments later, the wind gusted through the alley, nudging the constable's lifeless body. It swayed gently from the wall, like a lantern left burning long after its keeper was gone.

FOURTEEN

By the time Father Flynn arrived in town, the sun had sunk behind the frozen rooftops and the streets were glazed with evening frost. The lamps along High Street flickered to life, each a small defiance against the encroaching dark. Chimneys smoked like weary giants, and the glow of hearth-fires lit up the frosted windows, revealing silhouettes of families settling in for the long, cold night. The snow, which had begun as a polite flutter in the late afternoon, now came in fierce, blinding gusts—whirling down the narrow lanes so thick that one could barely see three paces ahead.

Flynn trudged up the icy cobbles, his cassock hem stiff with frost, and turned into *Ye Olde Knights of Jerusalem*. The familiar smell of ale, pipe smoke, and wet wool greeted him like a rough embrace. From the back room came the raucous sound of a choir mid-rehearsal for the Christmas Eve service at St. George's.

"*Fa-la-la-la-laaaaaaa, la-la-la-laaaaa!*" they sang—if one could call it that.

There was laughter, a few shoves, and the slosh of mugs being refilled. Cantor White, a serious fellow whose eyebrows seemed permanently furrowed in prayer or irritation, rapped his music stand with a spoon and barked, "Again, gentlemen! *Good King Wenceslas!* From the top!"

As Flynn removed his scarf, stamping the snow from his boots, he cast a glance around the smoky room. No sign of

Lord Dryden. Only the usual crowd of tradesmen and town officials, their conversation buoyed by drink. He took a seat by the window, hands clasped around a steaming mug of mulled ale, content to watch and listen.

At the opposite table, Levi Bairstow sat wedged between Colonel Blackwood and Adoniram Hedge. His waistcoat was tight, his smirk tighter still.

"Here we go again," he muttered, eyeing the choir with contempt. "Each one worse than the last. Sounds like a funeral for tone."

Adoniram grinned, raising his mug. "I like Christmas, I do. Reminds me o' me mum, God bless 'er, and the apples she used to give us on Christmas Day."

Bairstow turned to him with mock sweetness. "Do you like apples, Adi?"

"Aye," said Adoniram, confused but loyal. "Love 'em."

"Is that right?"

"Yeh."

Bairstow leaned closer, his voice dropping to a silken menace. "If I said I'd give you an apple for each time you spilled beer on that priest over there, what would you say?"

Adoniram followed the line of Bairstow's pointing finger to where Father Flynn sat, serene and unsuspecting by the fire. "That's it? Just spill beer?"

"That's it," said Bairstow.

"Why you wanna go makin' trouble for that stupid old priest, eh?"

Bairstow smirked. "Because, my dear Adi, he's Lord Dryden's pet Irish hound—sniffin' about, carryin' tales. And we can't exactly go spilling beer on a *lord*, can we?"

Blackwood sighed into his drink. "Come, Levi, must you rub it in? The man's harmless."

Bairstow turned his head, lazy as a snake. "If I wanted advice from you, my son, I'd ask."

"Never mind me, then," muttered Blackwood.

"I never do," Bairstow replied. "Now go on, Adi. Let's see if you've got the courage of a Christian."

Adoniram hesitated, clutching his glass. He looked around the pub, then shuffled to his feet and made his slow, reluctant way toward Flynn. The choir was midway through the first verse of *Good King Wenceslas*, their voices wobbling like drunks on ice.

Flynn sat quietly, reading from a small, leather-bound book. The candlelight gleamed off his spectacles. Adoniram approached, heart thudding, and cleared his throat.

"Father Flynn," he began, "is it true you're an Irishman?"

The choir stopped mid-note. The pub fell silent. Even the fire seemed to hesitate.

Flynn closed his book with deliberate calm, folded his hands in his lap, and looked up. His voice, when it came, was low and lilting.

"Did your father not thrash the muck outta you, Adi?" he asked. "Because this Father'd be happy to finish the job."

The men of *Ye Olde Knights of Jerusalem* erupted into laughter as Father Flynn, calm as a saint in a storm, stared straight ahead with a faint, knowing smile. His composure only deepened the room's amusement, though Adoniram Hedge's face had soured to a shade of beet.

"I'd like to see that, you old frail mick!" he barked, his voice cracking with both drink and humiliation. "You're practically knockin' on death's door!" He rapped his knuckles against the wooden post beside him and turned to grin at his brother Sam, who gave a guttural chuckle of approval.

Flynn rose slowly, setting his mug aside and slipping the small leather book into the pocket of his frock coat. "I must warn you, Mr. Hedge," he said, his voice steady as a sermon, "I'm a mite tougher than the little boys and women you and your brave brother take to smacking about at the mill—at the instruction of Levi Bairstow, no doubt."

"I would never!" Bairstow shot up from his chair, the protest rising from him like steam from a kettle.

Flynn's gaze did not shift. "Are you going to set down that glass and have your hide tanned by an old priest, or will you stand there bleating till the Almighty Himself grows tired of the sound?"

The laughter returned, sharper this time, the kind that pricks pride. Adoniram's jaw worked as though he were chewing stones. He glanced about the room, gauging sympathy, and finding none, turned half away as though to retreat—then spun suddenly, throwing a wild punch meant to catch Flynn unguarded.

But the old priest had seen his sort before—on the battlefield, in confession, and at the altar. In one deft motion, Flynn kicked the chair before him; it struck Adoniram square in the groin, folding the man forward like a penknife. Flynn's right fist rose in an upward arc—a perfect, priestly benediction—and connected cleanly beneath Hedge's nose.

The sound was obscene and oddly festive, like the popping of a champagne cork on Christmas Eve. Hedge went over backwards, limbs flailing, and hit the floorboards with a thud that rattled the pewter mugs.

Father Flynn straightened, clasped his hands behind his back, and revealed what he had gripped there all along—a stout wooden crucifix, polished by years of prayer.

"I saw that, Flynn!" cried Bairstow, leaping up, his face twisted with fury. "That ain't fair—you cracked him with that thing!"

Flynn turned to him, smiling. "I believe, Mr. Bairstow, in the power of the Cross."

The pub exploded into laughter once more, louder than before. Even Cantor White, poor man, who had tried to restore order to his carolers, was bent double behind the music stand.

Constable Blackwood, suppressing a grin, rose heavily and crossed to where Adoniram Hedge lay groaning. "Come on, Adi—you'll have to set that," he muttered. He knelt, pinched the broken bridge of Hedge's nose between thumb and forefinger, and yanked it sharply back into place. The resulting scream was nearly angelic.

Mayor Craig, leaning against the bar with the satisfied air of one watching divine justice unfold, raised his glass and chaser. "There now, lad," he called cheerily. "Up with you. Have a whiskey and an ale for the pain."

Blackwood hoisted the sniveling Hedge upright and steered him to the counter. Adoniram clutched a blood-soaked handkerchief to his face and, through watery eyes, downed the whiskey in one heroic gulp.

From the far end of the bar came a rasping voice, cracked with age and disdain. "Toughen up, you whining hussy," said

Mr. Cowley, his one good eye gleaming. "I've seen men wi' musket holes in 'em happier than you."

The pub fell silent. Even the fire seemed to hesitate in its crackle. No one spoke, no one laughed.

For years, Cowley had haunted the corners of *Ye Olde*, silent as a grave marker, nursing his ale and his ghosts. To hear him speak was rare enough—to hear him mock a Hedge was something close to divine intervention.

Flynn gave a single nod, as though in benediction, and sat down once more. The choir, after a long, uneasy pause, began again—softly this time.

"*Good King Wenceslas looked out…*"

And as the men's voices trembled through the smoke, the old priest smiled, warmed his hands at the fire, and murmured just loud enough for the nearest to hear, "Peace on earth, indeed."

Cowley turned back to his drink, muttering darkly into the foam. "Delicate little shite…"

Before anyone could reply, the door swung open, and a rush of cold air swept through the pub. In stepped Lord Dryden, tall and grave, his coat powdered white with snow, his expression set in stone. At once, half the pub stood as though a general had entered a barracks.

"Gentlemen," said Dryden, his tone clipped and weary, "as you were." He removed his gloves, setting them on the bar. "I've just been to see Widow Avondale."

A hush fell. Mayor Craig, always eager to sound official, broke it first. "A tragedy, my lord—aye, a most disagreeable bit of business. Perhaps the most disagreeable the town has ever seen. And just as Christmas draweth nigh."

The men murmured their assent. "Aye," came the collective sigh, followed by the lowering of eyes and the shaking of heads.

"Widow?" inquired Father Flynn quietly from his seat near the fire.

"The poor man fell into the well last night," said Constable Blackwood. "We found him at first light. Did you see Constable Whitehouse, sir?"

"I didn't," said Dryden, brow furrowing.

"Unlike him to miss choir practice," called out Cantor White from the back.

"Unlike him to miss *ale*, too," added Blackwood with a dry smile.

"Unlike him to miss a chance to annoy the life out o' everyone 'ere!" Levi Bairstow piped up, and the room broke into uneasy laughter.

The lord's gaze passed over the crowd until it landed on Adoniram Hedge, who sat at the bar holding a bloodied handkerchief to his swollen nose. "And what, pray, happened to you?" asked Dryden.

"He cheated!" Adoniram cried, pointing furiously at Flynn.

Dryden arched an eyebrow, a ghost of amusement flickering across his features. "He's Irish—of course he did."

The pub roared with laughter again, even Flynn himself managing a smile.

"Drink, sir?" asked the barkeep, Thomas Dilbert Gordon—a man so old that rumor had it he'd been serving drinks since before half the town was born.

"Guinness, Thom."

"Aye, my lord." Thom shuffled to the keg, humming a half-forgotten tune through his toothless gums. He began to pour, and as always, the stout overflowed the mug like a miniature flood.

"Thom," said Dryden sharply.

The old man blinked, realized his error, and fumbled to shut off the spout. The men at the bar grinned into their tankards. Thom's pace back to the counter was so slow it might have been mistaken for stillness.

Dryden accepted the mug, lifted it slightly, and took a measured sip. The firelight caught the stern lines of his face. "Is foul play suspected, Constable?" he asked at length.

"Not at present, sir," said Blackwood, straightening. "Dr. Blythe examined the body—no sign of force or struggle, save for the wound he took from the fall."

"Is he at Perely's?"

"Aye, sir."

Dryden nodded gravely. "Vicar Johnson is with the family. Three children. God help them this Christmas."

A moment of silence followed—broken only by the faint hiss of the fire and the scrape of a chair leg.

Then Levi Bairstow, clearing his throat with theatrical modesty, spoke up. "A collection will be taken by the merchants, my lord, and the factory shall donate a full month's wages to poor Mrs. Avondale."

A murmur of surprise rippled through the pub.

Levi placed a hand to his chest, crossing himself as though pained by memory. "And prayers will be offered tomorrow morn—for the soul of dear William. He was like a son to me, you know."

A few men exchanged glances, incredulous. Father Flynn's eyes narrowed slightly, but he said nothing.

Lord Dryden inclined his head. "Very generous of you, Mr. Bairstow. Well done, sir."

It cost him something to say it—every man in the room could see that—but he delivered the praise as one performs a civic duty, calm and exact. The men admired him for it. Only a man of Dryden's stature could compliment a scoundrel without surrendering an ounce of dignity.

Levi Bairstow bowed with the solemnity of a bishop, his expression carved in false humility. Blackwood and Hedge exchanged glances, astonished by his sudden piety. At the far end of the bar, Father Flynn muttered an oath beneath his breath and took a long, pointed sip of ale.

"Father," said Dryden, turning, "I'll need you to ride back with me."

Flynn looked down at his brimming glass as if it had betrayed him. "But… erm… I've only just—"

"Goodnight, gentlemen," said Lord Dryden firmly. "And a merry Christmas."

"Merry Christmas, sir," the men echoed in unison, their voices hushed with a kind of instinctive reverence.

Flynn followed Dryden out into the snow, grumbling under his breath. The two men climbed into the waiting carriage, drawing thick wool blankets around their legs as the coachman flicked the reins. The horses started off, their hooves clopping rhythmically through the snow.

They had not gone far before Dryden spoke, his tone low and deliberate. "We aren't going home, Flynn. We're going to find Diggy."

Flynn turned, startled. "Diggy? At this hour?"

"We must speak to him."

"He'll be three sheets to the wind by now, mark my words."

"Perhaps," said Dryden, coughing into his hand, "but Avondale's widow told me he's been coming to her door after midnight these past few nights—raving about seeing Tildon's ghost. She said the man was half-mad with it, put a chill in William's bones. Something about murder at the factory…" He trailed off, interrupted by another fit of coughing. "I didn't…"—another cough, harsher this time—"…really—"

His words stopped abruptly.

Flynn turned just in time to see the lord's eyes widen in horror as he doubled over, choking. A wet, crimson spatter struck the blanket between them. Then more. The sound was hideous—a bubbling gasp as blood poured from his mouth and nose, staining his tweed coat.

"Sweet Mary—" Flynn fumbled for him, but Dryden's body convulsed, his cough turning to a thick gurgle. Within moments, his head lolled forward.

Flynn threw open the carriage door, leaning half out into the storm. "Stop! Stop, I say! Stop!" he shouted, hammering on the roof with his fist.

The horses reared, and the carriage lurched to a halt. Flynn pulled himself back inside. Lord Dryden was slumped in the corner, motionless, eyes wide and glassy, mouth hanging open with blood still dribbling from the lip.

Flynn pressed two trembling fingers to the man's neck. No pulse. No breath.

The driver, Mr. Elby, clambered down from his perch and yanked open the door. His face went pale. "Good God, Father."

"Good God, indeed, Mister Elby."

"What is it?"

"I could be wrong," Flynn said grimly, wiping his bloodied hand on his coat, "but Dryden's been a healthy man. If it isn't a sudden hemorrhage—and it may be—it's poison."

"God help us," whispered the driver.

"Aye," said Flynn quietly. "With Jesus now. And may He help us uncover this devilry."

"Yes, sir."

"Ride into town. Find Doctor Blythe—he'll be at *Ye Olde*. Tell no one else, Elby—breathe not a word. If this be murder, the guilty party must not be warned. Take Blythe and the body to Perely's. I'll meet you there."

"Yes, Father."

And with that, Flynn stepped down into the snow and strode off along the dark road, his figure swallowed by the whirling white. Behind him, the carriage turned slowly, the lamps flickering in the storm.

Lord Dryden's body, still seated upright, swayed gently with each jolt of the wheels—its head nodding in eerie rhythm to the steady *jing-jing-jing* of the horses' bells as Mister Elby urged them on toward town.

FIFTEEN

The Headless Horseman was roaring that night—pipes smoked, boots clomped, and voices tangled like storm winds in the rafters. The air was thick with ale and gossip, for word had spread that Henry Dossett, the barkeep himself, had seen a ghost. And with poor William Avondale's body hauled out of the church well that very morning, most of the town now half-believed him.

On any other evening, Henry's story would've been laughed off as the ramblings of a drunken Scot. Bets would've been laid, shirtsleeves rolled, and someone—likely Henry—would've gone home with a split lip. But the snows had brought with them an eerie quiet, and the strange death of Avondale had settled over the town like a black veil. The laughter of the working class had turned to whispering; superstition, long dormant, began to stir again.

The door burst open, letting in a blast of cold air and a flurry of snow. In marched the Privateers, the gang of ragged factory boys, with Billy—cheeky, fearless Billy—strutting at the front.

"Line 'em up, Henry!" he cried, stamping the snow from his boots. "We're thirsty as 'ell!"

Henry blinked. "I don't know how ye do it, Billy."

Billy grinned, tossing a handful of coins onto the counter. "Easiest quid we ever made! The *Knights* feel sorry for us on account o' Til, I reckon—droppin' coppers in our 'ands easy as fallin' snow, they are."

The men around the bar laughed, though the mirth felt forced, like laughter in a graveyard.

Henry winced. "Good for you, lad—least one of us is high in spirits—" He stopped short, realizing his unfortunate choice of words. "Erm… you know what I mean." He busied himself pouring the boys' ale and whisky, his hands trembling slightly.

Billy looked around. "What's wrong wi' 'im?" he asked the room.

"He seen a ghost last night, Biww—haven't ye heard?" replied a man near the fire, puffing his pipe.

Billy turned sharply. "Ghost? Henry—is that true?"

Henry spun, his eyes wide and bloodshot. "As sure as I'm standin' right 'ere, Billy—William Avondale's ghost spoke to me."

The Privateers burst into laughter.

"You little rats," Henry barked, his voice rising. "I tell ye—it's true!"

"You're a bloody fibbin' Scot, 'Enry!" shouted Nicky 'Bug' Thatcher, a runt of a boy with a face blackened by soot and a grin that could split wood. The men roared with laughter again, raising their mugs as Bug took a proud swig.

Henry's expression darkened. He turned toward the great hearth, where an old musket hung above the mantle. "I swear upon my father's musket—Tessy Love, she's called—the same gun that choked ten rebels from the Colonies—I swear upon their lives and my father's, that William Avondale did enter this house last night and spoke to me."

The laughter died. The boys froze, mugs half-lifted. Even Bug lowered his drink. The wind howled outside, rattling the windows like fingernails.

FIFTEEN

After a long pause, Jimmy—nervous, thin Jimmy—spoke up in a small voice. "What did he want, Henry? Why'd he come here?"

Henry leaned over the counter, his eyes glinting in the lamplight. "He seeks his murderer, Jim. That's right—*murderer.*"

The word fell heavy as a hammer.

The boys stared, their bravado draining away.

"And I reckon," Henry went on, lowering his voice to a whisper, "he'll be back before long—maybe tonight—to ask what *you lot* might know." He pointed a trembling finger toward the boys, one by one. "So if any o' ye had a hand—or a tongue—that wronged William Avondale, best keep yer door barred and yer conscience clean."

No one laughed this time. The hearth crackled faintly. Somewhere outside, a shutter banged against the wind.

Billy swallowed hard and muttered, "You're daft, Henry." But his eyes flicked to the window, where snow pressed thick against the glass—white as the face of a ghost.

Henry had scarcely finished his last word when, without warning, every candle in *The Headless Horseman* went out at once. The room was plunged into blackness. For a moment there was only the sound of the wind pressing against the shutters—and then the faint hiss of cooling wicks.

Thin tendrils of smoke curled upward from the extinguished candles, drifting together, gathering in the center of the room. The pale vapors began to coil and turn, moving as though with purpose.

"What… the…" whispered Dicky Kimble, an old sailor who had seen too much of death at sea to startle easily.

The smoke thickened, swirling faster, until two distinct shapes began to emerge—shapes of men, outlined in a ghastly blue shimmer, their faces forming slowly like mist pressed into flesh.

The men of the pub gasped as one, the sound like the drawing of a single fearful breath. Every man recognized the faces. It was William Avondale and Constable Whitehouse.

Dicky stumbled back, crossing himself. "Get out, devils!" he shouted, fumbling for the knife he kept in his belt.

At his movement, the spectres opened their mouths wide—not as though speaking, but as if *inhaling*. From their throats came a terrible, drawn-out cry that seemed to pull the warmth from the room.

"*SILENCCCCCCCE, MORTALLLLLLLS!*"

The voice was deep and hollow, like wind howling through a tomb.

The Privateers shrieked, men dropped their mugs, and the smell of spilled ale mingled with cold smoke. No one moved.

Henry's voice quavered as he stammered, "W-w-w-william—I told the men… of your visitation… of your murder." His gaze shifted to the second ghost. "Philip—are we to believe that you are dead also?"

Whitehouse's spectre turned slowly toward him. The familiar good-natured grin he had worn in life was gone—replaced by a grotesque rictus. His eyes burned with unnatural light, their colors shifting like oil upon water. Wherever that gaze landed, men turned away, whimpering.

"*Myyyyy bodddddyyyyyy hangssssss ffffffrom thisssssss housssssssse…*"

"From here—the Horseman?" Henry whispered.

"*Ffffffrom thisssssss housssssssse!*" roared the ghost, his voice shaking the pewter mugs upon the shelves.

Then he turned sharply, fixing his terrible eyes upon the smallest of the Privateers. "*Jiiimmmmmmyyyyyy... weeeeeee haaaaaaave tillllll Chriiiiiiiiissstmaaaaaassssssss...*"

Jimmy's knees buckled, tears streaming down his grimy cheeks. "I'm sorry 'bout the carriage, sir..." he sobbed.

Whitehouse's mouth stretched into a scream that seemed to come from everywhere at once. "*Fffffffffind myyyyyy killerrrrrrrrrrrr!*"

"Ayyyyyyyyyyye," moaned Avondale, drifting closer beside him, "*Fffffffffind the killerrrrrrrrsssssss...*"

The two shapes rose higher, their voices melding into one dreadful command: "*Ffffffiiiiiiind themmmmm beeeeefore Chriiiiiiiiissssstmaaaaaaaassssss Daaaaaayyyyyyyy... orrrrrr beeeeeee trrroubled, visssitttttted... aaaaand hhhhhhhhunnn-ntttttted... Hhhhhhhhunnnttttted... Hhhhhunted... Hunted... Hunted...*"

The chant grew louder, overlapping until it seemed the very walls were speaking it.

Henry clutched the bar with both hands, shouting hoarsely over the din, "We'll find 'em! We will, I swear it!"

But the ghosts no longer heard him. They had become a cyclone of sound and light, repeating that single, dreadful word—

"*Hunted! Hunted! Hunted! Hunted! Hunted!*"

Each echo crashed through the room like a hammer-blow. Glasses shattered, men screamed, and then—

Silence.

The smoke collapsed inward and vanished, leaving behind only the stench of burnt tallow and the echo of that last word, whispering faintly through the rafters:

"*Hunted…*"

The men of the pub began to scream—some in terror, others in confusion—as chairs overturned and mugs shattered on the floor. The noise reached a feverish pitch, until, as suddenly as they had appeared, the ghosts were gone.

The blue glow vanished, leaving only a pall of smoke coiling where the spectres had been. The candles guttered back to life, dim and trembling, casting weak light across a room filled with pale faces. The men's cries faltered into sobs and gasps. Only the Privateers—poor factory lads, all trembling and blubbering—remained prostrate on the floor, facedown, hands clapped over their ears as though to keep the word *Hunted* from crawling back into their heads.

For a long moment, no one moved.

Then Dicky Kimble, the old sailor, lurched to his feet, his eyes bright with drink and something close to faith. He smashed his glass upon the ground—the sharp crack jolted the room like a musket report.

"Follow me, lads!" he commanded, drawing the knife from his belt.

The spell broke. The men, dazed and muttering, stumbled after him through the back of the pub, past the half-eaten pies and overturned stools, through the kitchen door and out into the snowy alley. The cold hit them like a slap.

"Tharr!" cried Dicky, pointing with his knife toward the stone wall beside the door.

Gasps rose from the men.

There, half-glazed with frost, hung Constable Whitehouse's body, limp and dusted white with snow, his face bluish, his boots scraping softly against the wall as the wind moved him.

"Tharr the dead sway," Dicky murmured, his voice trembling now.

The men fell back, crossing themselves, whispering prayers and curses alike. The horror of the thing was too plain to deny—their worst fears, frozen before them.

"What'll we do, then?" asked Bob Richards, a machine operator from the factory, his breath fogging in the cold.

"Leave it," said Henry, his voice steady though his hands shook. "Leave it there, and fetch the gentlemen of *Ye Olde*—lest they think we've had a hand in this mischief done to poor Whitehouse."

"What if it *is* one of us, Henry?" Richards asked, eyes darting toward the others. His voice cracked. "What if one o' the lads—?"

"Tisn't us," growled Dicky. "If it were, the ghosts would not have come. They've 'aunted *we* men to provoke *we* men to bring justice. I say the men of *Ye Olde* have sworn an oath with the Devil himself!"

"Calm yerself, Dicky," Henry snapped. "Not all the merchants could've done it. I've known some o' them all me life—good men, they are. But aye, I doubt you not—the murderer's among their ranks."

"Aye," Dicky muttered, "a mixed multitude, then…"

"How do we know *they've* not been 'aunted this very night, lads?" asked Jim Wesley, his face drawn and ghost-pale. "They might think *we're* to blame for Avondale's death! What if the same ghosts are whisperin' both sides into madness? What if it's the Devil's own trick—to pit town against town?"

"Aye," said another, shivering. "The Devil's work at Advent—to ruin Christ's birthday with fear and blood."

The men stared at the old sailor as he spoke, his voice lowering with each word until it was little more than a growl, the whites of his eyes flashing in the dark.

"To hell with the Devil," shouted Billy, stamping his foot. "If Father Flynn's anywhere about, he'll drive him out! We must fetch the priest!"

At once, a murmur of agreement rose. The mere mention of Flynn's name seemed to warm the air.

"Aye," said one, "fetch the Father—the Devil can't touch him, not if he's got the Elements."

Henry nodded, taking command. "Billy, can you and your lads run and bring Father back here?"

"Yes, sir!"

"Good. The rest of us'll wait here till you return."

Jim glanced toward the wall where the dead constable hung, his head tilted like a broken puppet. "What about the body, Henry? Shall we leave him to hang against the Horseman?"

"I don't like the omen," Dicky began, crossing himself. "The Devil's wor—"

"Leave it," Henry interrupted. "Father'll know what to do."

And so they stood in the swirling snow—the living and the dead—waiting on the priest, while the lamps of *The Headless Horseman* flickered faintly behind them like the last lights of a dying world.

SIXTEEN

Father Flynn spotted the shimmer of firelight dancing faintly through the trees ahead—a single pulse of warmth in the vast, frozen dark. His breath came in plumes as he trudged on, boots sinking into the deepening snow. The forest closed in around him, its branches heavy with white, bending low like mourners. The sound of his footsteps—*crunch, squawk, crunch*—was the only rhythm in that lonely wood until at last the little cabin appeared, its chimney spilling a crooked thread of smoke into the black sky.

He stumbled to the door and rapped hard with his knuckles. "Isaac! It's Flynn! Open, man!"

There was a shuffling sound from within, then a sliver of light as the door cracked open and a single bloodshot eye peered through the gap.

"Let me in, I'm freezing, Diggy!"

The door opened wider, and Flynn burst inside, stamping his boots and blowing warmth back into his hands. He made straight for the hearth, stretching his palms toward the fire.

Diggy—scruffy, wild-eyed, and barefoot—shut the door behind him. "Diggy's got mutton stew and a bottle—ye want?"

"Thank you, Isaac," said Flynn, teeth chattering, "but I don't think I could quite recover again from your mutton stew. I'm sure it brings nourishment to *your* body and soul, but it brings death and hellfire to mine. Too much pepper by half. I'll take my chances with the bottle."

"Diggy won't tell Bubs you said that," muttered the shepherd, moving toward the table. "Bubs is a proud king, he is."

"I've no doubt of it," Flynn said, smiling faintly. "And I hope His Majesty will accept my apologies."

Diggy grabbed a chipped cup, turned it upside down, examined the inside like a suspicious jeweler, then righted it and poured a hearty measure of dark rum. "Welcome to Diggy's 'ome, Father Flynn. You always been a friend to Diggy and Bubs. Friends are needed now—the dead needs friends, too."

Flynn frowned. "The dead, Isaac?"

Diggy nodded solemnly. "The dead, Flynn."

"What business have *you* with the dead?"

"Tisn't what Diggy's got with the dead," said the shepherd, eyes flickering toward the fire, "it's what the dead's got with Diggy."

Flynn drew nearer, lowering his voice. "Tell me, Isaac."

For a moment Diggy said nothing. He tipped the bottle to his lips and leaned back, swallowing deeply, his neck stretched like a sword-swallower's. The priest watched the firelight play across his rough, weather-beaten face.

"Well?" Flynn prompted gently.

Diggy set the bottle down with a dull thud. "Twas a week ago," he began, his voice rasping. "Diggy and Bubs were takin' the 'erd through the forest—back from shearin', near on dark. Snow was fallin'. Then it come. The blue boy."

Flynn's eyes narrowed. "The blue boy?"

"Aye," whispered Diggy. "The ghost boy. Little Til' Allen—the one laid to rest."

The priest's jaw tightened. "Go on."

Diggy's hands began to tremble. "Bubs and Diggy were scared near to death. Thought it was the Devil himself come collectin'—for the sins o' Diggy and Bubs. The boy was all light and mist, shinin' cold as moonwater, and he spoke no words. Just looked at me… oh, God…"

His voice cracked. He pressed his fists to his eyes and began to sob, shoulders heaving. "T'was for my sins, Father… sins for what I done… in the Colonies…"

Flynn leaned forward and laid a hand on the man's back. "There now, Isaac," he said softly. "You're fine, lad. The Lord's mercy is greater than the Devil's debt. And what does Bubs have to do with this? What are his sins?"

"Bubs don't go to Mass."

"He's a sheep, Isaac."

"And a pagan."

"Right." Flynn swallowed a smile and scream.

Diggy gathered himself, wiping his sleeve across his face. For a moment he sat in silence, staring into the fire—the flames dancing across his wet cheeks, the light catching in his wild eyes. Then, with sudden force, he slammed his palm against the table.

"We ain't fine, Flynn!" he shouted, voice breaking. "We *ain't!*"

Flynn leaned forward, startled. "Why aren't ye fine, Isaac?"

Diggy choked on another sob, his whole frame shaking. "Diggy run."

"Run? What do ye mean, ye run?"

"Diggy run at the battle," he said, eyes far away now, as though watching some distant field. "Left Diggy's friends t' die—and die they did. Whole regiment, cut down like sheep in the snows. Blood on the snows, death on the snows…" He rocked as he spoke, muttering, "They come in me dreams, the lads—faces red as the snow is white…"

Flynn crossed himself quietly. "So what of these ghosts, Isaac?"

Diggy's gaze darted to the fire again. "Diggy told the boy ghost," he whispered, "and the boy ghost told Diggy he were *pushed*—pushed, Flynn!—and that Diggy must find the pusher. Said Diggy wouldn't be coward no more, nor 'aunted, if Diggy helped."

Flynn's brows drew together. "You say the boy was *pushed*? Did Tildon tell you that, plain as day?"

"He were, Flynn," Diggy insisted, nodding violently. "He were! And Diggy must help Til—Diggy *promised!*"

Flynn exhaled slowly, steadying his voice. "And is this what you went to tell William Avondale?"

"Aye," Diggy said, sniffing. "Avondale were told—bloody man wouldn't suffer Diggy a moment. Called me names, he did. Sent Diggy and Bubs away, like dogs."

Flynn frowned. "Avondale was found dead this morning—at St. George's Well."

The shepherd's head jerked up. "Dead?"

"Dead, Isaac."

Diggy's face went pale. "He's been here," he whispered. "He, and Til, and the Constable, and Lord Dryden."

Flynn's mouth fell open. "Constable?"

"Aye," Diggy said, voice trembling. "They was all here before ye come barging in—come outta the fire they did, blue as candle flame, beggin' for right done by 'em. Twas a terrible bloody sight." He paused, then gave a strange, watery chuckle. "And a good laugh, too."

Flynn blinked. "A laugh?"

"Aye," Diggy said, a half-smile creeping through his tears. "Til told Diggy a joke. The dead tell jokes, ye know."

"Ha!" Flynn barked, shaking his head. "Well, Isaac, it seems the task o' settlin' this restless lot has fallen to you and me—and Bubs, of course. Where do we start?"

Diggy thought for a long moment, chewing his lip, his eyes fixed on the fire as though it might answer for him. Then he looked up. "To the *Horseman*," he said at last. "The poor 'ave been told the news first. The rich'll hear it soon enough."

Flynn rose, pulled his cloak about his shoulders, and nodded gravely. "Then to the *Horseman* we go. Heaven help us, Isaac. Heaven help us all."

SEVENTEEN

On the outskirts of town, beneath a sky heavy with drifting snow, Father Flynn and Diggy trudged through the frost-bitten fields toward the dim lights of Stratford. It was near midnight when they were met by the Privateers, huddled together like a pack of frightened foxes. Their faces were pale, their breath visible in the dark.

They poured out the tale at once—the ghosts that had appeared at the *Horseman*, the dreadful discovery of Constable Whitehouse's body, and the things that had been said by the men inside the pub.

When they had finished, Billy stepped forward nervously. "D'ye bring the cross an' holy water, Father?"

Flynn smiled faintly beneath his breath, the ghost of humor softening his lined face. "I always carry my cross, lad," he said, patting his breast. "But I haven't any holy water—and I won't need it. Ye can't baptize a ghost, nor does an apparition need the cross. These aren't vampires or werewolves, boys—this is the *innocent blood of Abel* crying out over the land."

The boys blinked at him in silence until Bug, the smallest, piped up. "Who's Abel, Father?"

"Abel," said Flynn, leaning down toward him, "was the first man murdered—by his own brother, at that."

"How'd he get it?" asked another boy.

"His skull was caved in by a rock," said Flynn gravely.

The lads gave a collective *"ew"*—half horror, half fascination.

Bug was the first to find his tongue. "What cause did his brother have for killin' 'im?"

"Cain was jealous," Flynn answered. "Abel was blessed, and Cain was not. Greed and envy, lads—the two surest ways to make devils of men."

Bug swallowed. "Was Til murdered for envy then?"

Flynn's eyes darkened. "I don't know, Bug—but we'll find out."

Bug hesitated, then whispered, "Is Til a demon?"

"No, lad," said Flynn. "He ain't a demon. He's a troubled spirit—unsettled, restless, waitin' for peace to fall upon the town. He visited ye not to harm, but to warn—to *save* life, not take it."

Bug frowned. "How're ye sure he ain't a demon, Father?"

Flynn chuckled softly, though there was no mirth in it. "Because demons are cowards, boy. They hide behind shadows and make their mischief unseen. They'd rather whisper their poison than face a soul made new. Ghosts, though—they've no deceit in 'em. They come to make truth known, not hide it."

The lads looked uneasy. "So we should fear the ghosts," one ventured, "and not the demons?"

Flynn straightened, his breath clouding before him. "Nay—fear the ghosts, in the way a wise man fears judgment. *Listen* to what they've said. But as for demons—no, lads. Fear them not. They can do nothing to the dead in whom the *Resurrecting Spirit* dwells."

Bug tilted his head. "To the dead? Are we the dead, Father?"

Flynn's eyes twinkled. "Have ye been baptized, Bug?"

"Aye," the boy said proudly.

"Then you're dead," Flynn replied, grinning. "Holy water drowned ye at baptism—and it drowns your memory of sin every time ye remember it. You're dead to sin, lad, which is why the Spirit can live in ye at all. So if the same Spirit that raised Christ from the dead dwelleth in ye," he added, drawing the sign of the cross in the frosty air, "then demons, my boys—demons are scared *piss-less* of ye."

The Privateers exchanged glances—half amazed, half emboldened—and Billy whispered, "Then God help the devils tonight."

Flynn's eyes glinted in the moonlight. "Aye, lads. God help 'em indeed."

The boys laughed—nervous laughter at first, then freer—and were comforted by the priest's grin and the warm, iron certainty in his voice.

"So we don't 'ave to be a'feared o' Til's ghost, then?" asked Billy, kicking at a lump of snow.

"Nor of any ghost," said Father Flynn, "nor of any demon, nor of any other created thing. The Spirit that made all things dwelleth in ye—"

"Didn't help Til, tho, did it?" interrupted Bug, his small voice cracking. "Nor William, nor Whitehouse…"

Flynn's tone softened. "Death is inevitable, lad—fear is optional. Death is not final, which is why ye've got the right to resist fear. Consider yerselves dead *to* fear and alive *to* Christ."

"Alive to the baby?" Bug piped, smirking, and the others snorted into their sleeves.

Flynn chuckled. "Aye—alive to the baby, if ye like. Every man in this town's walkin' about afraid o' death. If they think on death, they piss themselves; if they don't, they dismiss themselves. It's piss or dismiss, lads—piss or dismiss!"

The boys roared with laughter, doubling over in the snow. Even Diggy snorted, though he tried to hide it.

Father Flynn grinned wide and raised his fist, the moonlight glinting off his spectacles. "Christ dealt with the fear of this town long ago. He walked straight up to the biggest bully in the schoolyard"—he swung his arm wide, cutting the air with a great whoosh—"and smashed him right in the face—*death!*"

The boys whooped and cheered.

"Your Christian names and baptisms aren't some fairytale joke," Flynn went on, his voice now a rolling thunder. "You are *Englishmen*—Christian, born into courage, unafraid of death! All of England belongs to Christ and Christians. You are young English lions—not of the factory, but of the town itself—demanding justice and devourin' the works o' the devil!"

At that, Bubs the sheep, who had been trailing behind with Diggy, gave a loud, indignant *baa.*

"It's all right, Bubs," Diggy muttered gravely. "Diggy don't like lions neither."

The boys collapsed into laughter again, the sound carrying through the cold air like a hymn of mischief.

As they approached the dim glow of *The Headless Horseman*, the laughter faded. The firelight through the windows was low and trembling. Flynn's voice dropped to a near whisper. "Where's the body?"

The boys led him down the narrow alley behind the pub. Snow had drifted high against the walls, and the wind whistled through the cracks like a ghost's breath.

"There," said Billy, pointing.

Father Flynn stepped closer and peered upward. The body of Constable Whitehouse hung stiffly against the back wall, the wire cutting deep into his neck, his face pale and frozen. Flynn examined the garrote, tracing the taut line upward to the eaves. Then he rapped on the back door.

It opened to reveal Jim Wesley, pale as flour.

"Has anyone been on the roof?" asked Flynn.

"Nay, not yet," answered Henry, appearing behind him. "We've waited for ye, Father."

Flynn nodded grimly. "We cannot move the body until we've searched above. We'll need daylight for that. Best you men go home and get what rest ye can. We'll reconvene before daybreak. I'll alert Constable Blackwood—my next business lies at *Ye Olde.*"

"How'll any of us sleep?" Henry asked, his voice low. "We're terrified."

"Aye," echoed the others. "Not a wink between us."

Flynn studied their faces, weary and haunted in the flickering light. "Then stay here," he said gently. "Stay, and pray. And think—think hard—who among this town would have reason to do such a thing."

He pulled his cloak tight and stepped back into the storm. "I'll return before the dawn, once I've delivered the news."

And with that, Father Flynn strode into the dark, his figure swallowed by the snow, while behind him the men of the *Horseman* huddled together—watchful, whispering, and waiting for the night to end.

EIGHTEEN

Father Flynn entered *Ye Old Knights of Jerusalem* at half past midnight, the sound of the door creaking open briefly silencing the room before the laughter and clatter resumed. The choir had long since abandoned their carols and were now gathered around a table in the back, shouting over a raucous game of cards. Bairstow, Blackwood, and Sam Hedge were in their usual booth, surrounded by a battalion of empty glasses that glistened under the lamplight. Mayor Craig and several merchants occupied the next booth, chuckling heartily at some bawdy tale about a pig, a bishop, and a barn fire.

Old Thom, stationed faithfully behind the bar, was polishing a mug with his ancient rag—moving, as ever, at a speed that made glaciers seem impatient. He looked up as Flynn entered, nodded a greeting, and shuffled toward the tap. The sound of ale pouring into a glass was like a hymn to Thom, slow and steady, reverent.

"Welcome back, Father," said Mr. Herbert William Heathrow of the Mayport and Carlisle Railway, raising his own glass with the indulgent cheer of a man too deep in drink to stand.

"Back?" inquired Vicar Johnson, who was leaning against the bar with one elbow. "Had to kick him out again, hey Thom?"

"I don't think anyone could kick Flynn out of a pub, Vicar," said Thom in his raspy monotone without looking up.

The men laughed, and the noise swelled once more.

"Heard what you did to Adoniram's nose, Father," Heathrow continued with a grin. "Is that how they teach the faith in Dublin these days?"

Flynn smiled faintly as Thom handed him his pint. "We Catholics," he said, "believe in a sort of holistic discipleship, Mr. Heathrow. And as a good priest, I didn't wish to spoil Mr. Hedge by sparing the rod."

The table erupted in laughter, and even Vicar Johnson cracked a smile.

"Good show, Flynn," Heathrow said, pounding the bar. "Terrific!"

Johnson shook his head, chuckling. "You're an impossible man, Flynn."

"So I'm often told," the priest replied, raising his glass in a modest salute.

The room hummed with easy warmth, but Flynn's eyes had already begun to wander, quietly cataloging the faces before him. Who had stayed since he last left? Who was still drinking? Who looked too calm for comfort? Bairstow appeared as composed as ever, sipping his ale and whispering to Sam Hedge, whose nose was freshly bandaged and whose pride was not. Blackwood was watching the card table with feigned amusement, though his brow furrowed every few moments. The merchants were loud and careless, their laughter rolling through the smoke like the ringing of cracked bells.

Flynn took a slow sip of his ale. No whispers followed him, no cautious glances. Not a soul seemed to suspect what had happened to Lord Dryden. Could the poison have been accidental? Or had the Lord's death been the hand of nature—an unseen weakness of the heart, perhaps?

He thought of Blythe's autopsy still to come. If the doctor found traces of poison, it would confirm what Flynn already feared—that the deaths were connected. Avondale, Whitehouse, Dryden—each one tied by some invisible thread that wound through this very room.

If the murderer was still here, they were brilliantly composed. Too composed. He scanned again, the wheels in his mind turning.

Or perhaps, he thought, setting his mug down, the murderer had already gone home.

He looked toward the door, half-expecting it to open again. Who was missing from before?

Cowley.

Adoniram.

Cantor White.

Father Flynn repeated the names quietly to himself, committing them to the dim vault of his memory. He drew a small leather notebook from his waistcoat and, with his pencil poised, wrote a brief circle of notes—names, times, odd turns of phrase overheard—then snapped it shut and slid it back into his coat. He took a slow sip of ale, cleared his throat, and looked round the room.

"Gentlemen—may I have your attention, please?"

The chatter fell to a low hum and then died away altogether. The smoke from the lamps hung in the air like a curtain. Flynn walked into the centre of the room, his boots sounding sharply against the oak floorboards.

"You gonna sing us a tune, then, Flynn?" came Levi Bairstow' voice from his table, loud and oily. The men roared with laughter.

Flynn smiled faintly and waited, his hands behind his back, until the noise subsided.

"Sirs," he began evenly, "it is my unfortunate duty to inform you that Constable Whitehouse has been found dead this night—hanged by the neck. His body still dangles, lifeless, from the roof of *The Headless Horseman.*"

The room erupted. Gasps, curses, the scrape of chairs on wood. Constable Blackwood shot to his feet, his face drained of colour.

Flynn raised a hand for quiet. "And—gentlemen—there will be time to examine the body. As I said, he yet hangs where he was found. I have reason to believe that not a soul down at the Horseman bears guilt in this affair. They are sore afraid and have sent me here to inform Constable Blackwood and the rest of you at once."

The door of *Ye Olde Knights of Jerusalem* burst open before he could continue. A gust of snow and freezing wind swept through the pub, extinguishing two candles and causing the lanterns to flicker wildly. All heads turned as a figure entered—tall, wrapped in a dark greatcoat, face hidden beneath a wool scarf.

The door slammed behind him, and for a moment only the howling of the wind outside was heard. The newcomer turned his back to the crowd, unwrapping his scarf and shaking the snow from his shoulders. He hung his coat deliberately on the rack, then turned round to reveal a pale, tired face—Dr. Horace Harland Blythe.

"Good evening," he said.

"Good evening," the room murmured in unison, uncertainly.

Blythe crossed to Flynn, his boots leaving wet prints on the floorboards, and bent close to whisper in the priest's ear. His words were brief but grave; Flynn's brow furrowed, and his expression changed to one of stunned comprehension. Realizing that the whole pub was watching, Blythe retreated a step and gave a faint, awkward smile to the room.

Flynn turned back to the assembly. His voice, when he spoke, had lost its clerical calm. "I fear," he said slowly, "that the worst news is yet to come." He paused, eyes downcast, then lifted his head. "Lord Dryden is dead."

The silence that followed was thick and absolute. Men rose from their seats as if compelled by some invisible hand.

"Saints," whispered the vicar, his face ashen. "I was only just with him, Flynn. What is this—how?"

"What the devil is going on in this town?" barked Constable Blackwood, his voice trembling with fury.

"Flynn?" the vicar said again, appealing to him. "Men, please—Flynn must be allowed to speak."

Flynn stood there in the stillness, his hand resting on the back of a chair, the firelight flickering across his face, preparing to tell them what he feared to say aloud.

Father Flynn nodded slowly, letting the room still before he spoke. "When Lord Dryden and I left here some hours gone, we were halfway home in his carriage. He'd been speakin' of Isaac Digby—ye know, the shepherd with the mad sheep—when he started coughin'. At first, I thought little of it. But the cough turned to blood. Before the coachman could pull up, the poor man was spittin' red and choking on it. He was gone within minutes."

A hush fell like frost over the room. Flynn went on, his tone grave but steady. "I had the carriage turned round and sent straight to Dr. Blythe. From the first, I suspected foul play. Ye all know Lord Dryden—fit as a fiddle, a ridin' man, sound in wind and limb. There was no earthly ailment in him that I'd ever known."

He paused to let that sink in. The fire popped. Someone coughed.

"After leavin' the body to Blythe's care, I made my way to Isaac Digby's cottage. Before his death, Lord Dryden had told me Isaac had been haunterin' William Avondale—botherin' him for three days about young Tildon Allen's fall, swearing the lad was murdered."

"Bollocks!" roared Levi Bairstow, slamming his mug so hard the ale jumped. "The lil' brat fell of 'is own bloody accord, Flynn, ye filthy, loose-tongued mick!"

Flynn's eyes flashed like iron under a forge. "I'll knock yer block clean off, Bairstow, if ye open that mouth again."

"Good God, Flynn!" cried Mayor Craig, half rising.

Levi leaned back, fuming, but said no more. His jaw worked like a bull readying for charge.

Flynn's Irish would come through all the more fierce when he was stirred. He shot back, "I'm not layin' blame on any soul here," Flynn continued coolly. "I'm tellin' ye what I know. And what I *know* grows blacker by the hour."

"Go on, Father," muttered Old Thom from behind the bar.

"So," Flynn said, pacing a little, "I went to Isaac's, and the man swore he'd seen ghosts."

Levi let out a bark of laughter. "Ghosts? Oh, spare us yer

churchyard tales! Diggy's got more gin than guts in him, and that stupid sheep's got more sense than the both o' ye!"

"Silence, Levi!" thundered Constable Blackwood, standing now. His voice cracked the laughter like a whip.

Flynn turned his gaze on the crowd. "No jest, I tell ye. Isaac said he saw the ghost o' Tildon Allen—and without knowin' Whitehouse was dead, he said he saw *his* ghost, too."

A tremor passed through the men. Someone crossed himself.

"When I came back into town to inquire after Lord Dryden," Flynn went on, "I was met by the Privateers. They led me to the Horseman, where I saw Whitehouse hangin' cold from the roof. The sight near froze my blood—it gave weight to Digby's tale. The men there told me they'd been visited this very night by the ghosts o' Tildon Allen, William Avondale, and Philip Whitehouse."

He looked round the room. "Thirty-two men, sober enough to swear it."

"What did they say, Father?" asked Thom quietly.

"That they'd been murdered, every one of 'em—and know not by whose hand. They warned that others are bein' hunted even now." Flynn's voice deepened, and his eyes swept toward the bar where Bairstow sat rigid. "And if ghosts can't find peace till justice's done, then God help whoever's hidin' in the light."

He let that hang, then finished, quieter still:

"But there's a plainer matter than ghosts. By the use of reason—and by the science of Dr. Blythe—it can be known Lord Dryden was poisoned. And the poison was served *in this very house.*"

"Are ye completely in yer right mind, Flynn?" asked the Vicar, half in disbelief and half in genuine concern.

"I've never been *more* in me right mind, nor more convinced that somethin' foul's afoot, Vicar," replied Flynn, his brogue thickening as he warmed to his subject. "Ask the good Doctor there—Blythe—was he not poisoned?"

Blythe inclined his head solemnly. "He was."

Flynn spread his hands. "And what was the poison used?"

"Unmistakably cyanide," answered the Doctor.

Flynn turned back to the room, his voice rising. "Cyanide, gentlemen—a foolish mistake, but a tellin' one. *Telling,* I say, in that the murderer was here tonight, in *this very house,* as cyanide's fast actin'. Dryden didn't live ten minutes after it hit his blood."

"If it's *fast actin',*" barked Levi Bairstow, leaning forward, red-faced, "'ow're we to know it weren't you that poisoned 'im, Flynn? You was wiff 'im when 'e died, weren't ye?"

The room shifted uneasily. A few men murmured, a few nodded, others frowned. Flynn did not move.

"Because," said the priest, slow and steady, his eyes moving from face to face, "I believe all these recent deaths are related. And what's more, I believe we'll find answers when we take Whitehouse down tomorrow and examine the roof—"

"Tomorrow!?" shouted Blackwood, slamming a fist on the table. "The man ought to be taken down immediately!"

"Constable Blackwood," said Flynn, lifting a hand, "do what ye see fit. But the night's dark, and the snow's comin' in sheets. The wires from which he dangles must be examined carefully if we're to learn anythin'. And it's my judgment,"—he looked round the room—"that we first treat this very pub as a crime scene. We must recollect, right now, who was here while Lord Dryden sat among us, and who left after him. Forget, for the moment, the business o' ghosts—Dryden's been murdered, and I'd wager Whitehouse has too. I suggest we work backwards—from Dryden, to Whitehouse, to Avondale if needs be—and take no counsel from the ale or the afterlife."

He leaned forward, voice sharpening. "We are men o' reason, not superstition. I've seen no ghost, and even if I had, I'd not throw my wits to the wind because a candle flickered or wine made my heart soft."

Levi smirked. "Why the 'ell are you a Catholic, then?"

Flynn shot him a look that could have stripped paint. "Because we *created* the University, ye thundering bank account."

Laughter rippled through the room, easing the tension for a moment.

"Right, Flynn," said Blackwood, clearing his throat. "I'm with you—provided we get Whitehouse down at first light. And you men here'll come as well."

"I'm also with you, Flynn," added the Vicar. "Let's make up the list now, gentlemen. Thom, have you parchment and pencil?"

Thom blinked, then bent beneath the bar, producing a sheet of paper and a stub of English lead.

"Give it here, Thom," said Mayor Craig. "And pour us another ale while you're about it."

"Here, too," called a voice.

"Aye, aye," Thom muttered, shuffling down the counter with glacial patience.

The mugs were refilled, and the men leaned close as Craig began to jot down names—those present when Dryden had been in the room, and those who'd left since. It was then suggested that another list be made: the men who'd stood nearest the bar, closest to where Dryden had drunk his final pint.

When Craig had finished, he set the lead aside and handed the list to the Vicar, who began to read aloud. Flynn listened, but his mind wandered. He thought of the names he himself had written earlier in his small notebook—Old Cowley, Cantor White, Adoniram.

Maybe it wasn't one of them. Maybe it was. Maybe the killer sat still among them now, nursing his ale and waiting for the dawn.

Someone asked if any man had come behind the bar that night. Thom straightened, affronted. "No," he said flatly. "No one. Never do I let another soul behind my bar."

The men believed him without question. Thom's slowness of service was so well known it had become a proverb in the town: *Slow as Thom's pour at Ye Olde.*

And for once, that slowness served him well.

The hour had grown heavy, and even the lamps in *Ye Olde* seemed to burn lower, their light bowing before the coming dawn. Flynn, rubbing the bridge of his nose, suggested that the men go home and rest before meeting again at the *Horseman* at seven o'clock sharp. There were grumbles, but agreement all the same; exhaustion had at last conquered curiosity. One by one, they filed out into the snow, their boots crunching on the frozen street, voices low and wary. Only old Thom remained behind, polishing the same glass he had been working at since nine o'clock, indifferent to murders, mysteries, or men.

Flynn stepped out into the cold, the night air cutting clean through his coat. He lit his pipe, the flame from his match flaring briefly against the darkness, and began the slow walk toward the *Horseman.* The street was utterly still, save for the hiss of falling snow and the occasional groan of a shutter in the wind. His mind roamed in circles—Dryden, Whitehouse, Avondale, Tildon—threads of death weaving themselves through the same cursed town. The smoke from his pipe rose and twisted like the ghosts Diggy swore he'd seen.

When Flynn reached the *Horseman*, he found the door unlatched. He stepped inside without hesitation. The familiar warmth struck him first—the heavy smell of ale and oak, the low crackle of the hearth. A handful of men had remained behind, too fearful to face the long road home alone. They greeted him quietly, relief softening their eyes as he unwrapped his scarf and hung his coat on the hooks by the door.

Henry Dossett was crouched by the hearth, feeding the fire. He looked up and nodded. "Take the large chair in the corner, Father. There's a horse blanket in the back—I'll fetch it for ye."

"Thank ye, Henry," said Flynn through the side of his mouth, pipe between his teeth. "Though I may be asleep before ye bring it. It's been quite a night."

"Aye—it has," Henry murmured, setting another log to the blaze.

Flynn sank into the chair beneath the mounted head of a deer—its glassy eyes staring into eternity—and stretched his legs toward the fire. He puffed once more on the pipe, then let his eyes close. Within moments, the room filled with the soft, strangled music of his snoring—a peculiar sound halfway between a duck being throttled and a bagpipe leaking air.

The men smiled, quietly, exchanging glances over their tankards. It was strangely comforting to hear the old priest's dreadful snore. His presence, more than the fire or the ale, lent them courage. If Father Flynn could sleep, then perhaps the night itself could be trusted again.

One by one, the others followed suit. Henry preferred the company this night so he didn't rush anyone out. The Privateers—Billy, Bug, and the rest—curled up before the hearth upon a patchwork of animal hides so old and many that no man could count their number. The older men reclined in their chairs, which creaked and sighed like ancient bones each time one of them shifted.

Soon, the room had settled into a chorus of heavy breathing and muted snores, the dying fire painting their faces in gold and ember-red. Outside, the snow fell softly, muffling the world. Inside, only the priest and the boys truly slept.

NINETEEN

At precisely 6:55 in the morning, Constable Blackwood rapped on the back door of *The Headless Horseman.* The sound echoed down the narrow alley like the knock of judgment itself. Inside, Henry had already been up an hour, cracking eggs over a sputtering griddle and keeping half an eye on a pot of porridge that threatened to boil over. The air hung thick with smoke and the sharp smell of pork burnt to a char. A few of the men—those who hadn't slept at all—sat bleary-eyed around the tables, coughing and waving the haze from their faces.

Father Flynn, still wrapped in the black horse blanket that served as his bed and vestment both, rose from his chair with a grunt and shuffled to the door. When he opened it, the early light poured in around Blackwood's pale face.

"Coffee?" moaned the Constable, his voice rough and low.

"Mary's Angel—ye don't look like ye slept a wink," Flynn replied, blinking against the light. "In fact, ye don't look like ye *left Ye Olde* last night. You're white as a sheet!"

"Come here, Constable," called Henry from the bar. "Get somethin' in yer belly."

Blackwood trudged over as Henry set out a plate and, with the authority of a general, commanded, "Eat that," before sliding a giant mug of Guinness across the bar. "And drink this."

"For breakfast?" asked Blackwood, eyeing it with suspicion.

"Have ye ever been to Ireland, Constable?" said Flynn, pulling out his pipe but not lighting it.

"I can't say that I 'ave."

"Best way to start the mornin'," Flynn replied.

Blackwood looked from one to the other, waiting for a laugh that didn't come. Finally, he sat down and began to eat, tearing through the eggs and burnt pork like a man starved. When he had finished the plate and drained the mug, he straightened his collar, cleared his throat, and assumed his most official manner.

"I hope you gentlemen understand," he began solemnly, "that my judgment in this matter of Whitehouse—specifically regarding the culpability of this establishment—cannot, and will not, be swayed by a morning breakfast, as delicious as it were, Henry."

Flynn and Henry exchanged a glance and then nodded, faces drawn into exaggerated seriousness. "Course not—'a course not," they echoed, trying not to grin.

Blackwood, satisfied, turned toward the room and announced, "Shall we?"

The men rose slowly, stretching and shrugging into their coats. Outside, the dawn was painting the rooftops in gold, and the snow had taken on a pinkish hue under the first light of day. Mayor Craig and Vicar Johnson appeared at the end of the street, their breath rising in clouds as they approached.

A moment later, the tap-tap of a walking stick sounded against the bricks. Around the corner came Levi Bairstow, with the Hedge brothers on either side of him, all three dressed too fine for the hour. Bairstow struck his cane along the wall of *The Headless Horseman* as they passed, each tap ringing clear as a warning bell in the cold morning air.

"I'm 'ere to see no evidence be planted by Flynn here an' his two or three witnesses," Levi announced, cane tapping the stones with officious rhythm. Blackwood merely rolled his eyes and waited for the men to settle.

"All right, Levi. All right—nobody's blamin' you just yet," Flynn shot back, calm as wind.

Dickie Kimble, patch over one eye and pint balanced on his palm, spat a frosty laugh. "We must wait fer the full sun to be seen afore the body be touched or moved—so as to give the Devil time to fly or be scorched."

Flynn laughed outright; Vicar Johnson's chuckle joined it, thin and bright. "The Devil don't live in dead bodies, ye silly piss," Flynn said, and the word landed like a stone. Johnson guffawed; Dickie cursed and took a deliberate sip—then, with a barked oath, dumped the rest of his pint into the snow.

"I'll not drink with pagans masqueradin' as men o' the Cross," the old sailor grumbled.

Flynn rolled his eyes, "Dickie—God love ya—you wouldn't know the Cross 'were ya nailed to it."

"Why'd you pour that out, Dickie?" Jimmy blurted. "I'd'a drank that!"

"Better be sober as a judge than drink with the Devil, boy," Dickie replied, eyes wild as cut glass.

Levi's cane began its impatient percussion on the wall again. "Alright, alright," Blackwood said at last. "Henry—give us a ladder."

Henry obliged with a ladder, heavy as a sin and smelling of sap. They leaned it against *The Headless Horseman's* eaves. Up climbed Blackwood, slow and cautious; behind him climbed

Flynn, the Vicar, and—despite himself—Levi Bairstow, cane tucked under his arm like a swaggering ensign.

Blackwood pointed with a gloved hand to a length of wire coiled round the chimney and stretched down the sloping tiles. "The cords that hung John Tawell," he muttered, an ugly little smile creasing his face.

Flynn crouched to inspect the coils. "The wire's a double knot—a garrote," he said, voice low. "And telegraph wire doesn't wrap itself five times round a chimney, fall off a building the perfect length o' a man's neck, and make a garrote all by itself."

The Vicar looked alarmed. "Blackwood—you do catch Flynn's meanin', don't you? That this knot was set up by human hands?"

"Aye," the constable answered gravely.

"And what's more," Flynn continued, "hands that have acquired knowledge o' an assassin's rope." He glanced at the men below. "To be sure."

Levi shifted, offended and yet unnerved. Flynn turned his back on him and called gently, "You're almost entirely not the man we'd be after, Levi."

"Why's that?" Levi snapped.

"Because you're neither hard enough nor smart enough to have done this," Flynn said simply. There was a steel under his placid voice now that made Levi's jaw set.

"Cut him down—grab his body down there, lads!" Blackwood barked. The men at the foot of the ladder caught the wire as the constable severed it; Whitehouse's frozen bulk slipped downward, arms rigid, eyes glazed as river-ice. They eased him onto a cart, wrapping him in sacking and blankets with a clumsy tenderness.

NINETEEN

They wheeled the body to Dr. Blythe's at once. The Doctor worked with his measured calm: examination, notes, the cold precision of one accustomed to the commerce of death. When he spoke at last, his words were like winter—clear and hard. The cause of Whitehouse's death: asphyxiation. Time of death: about sixteen hours prior. Blackwood crosschecked a telegraph engineer's log and confirmed the wire had been down since roughly two o'clock the previous afternoon.

Flynn let the numbers settle into him like snow into cloth. The chronology mattered. A killer had set things in motion long before anyone had noticed, long before the pub's carols or the boys' pranks. The murderer had thought to conceal, to time, to manipulate.

While the men stood in the cold and cursed softly and spat tobacco and smoke, Flynn felt the weight of one more duty press in upon him. He wrapped the black horse blanket about his shoulders, stepped past the shuttered door of *The Headless Horseman*, and turned his face toward Stratford Hall. The road lay white and long ahead, tracks already dimming in the falling snow. He thought of Catherine—young, fierce, and ignorant of this new horror—and his chest tightened. There was a terrible kindness in the telling that must be done.

He mounted the hired pony at the livery, set his cap deep, and rode into the grey morning, the bells of the town still muffled, his thoughts full of lists and names and the hard, surgical necessity of truth.

TWENTY

Catherine Dryden sat in her father's library, the one room in Stratford Hall that still carried the scent of him—tobacco, leather, and faintly, gunpowder. Her back was to the doorway through which Father Flynn entered. She sat curled in her favorite chair: a worn, buttoned Italian leather seat her father had favored for his long readings of Aquinas. The chair was placed just beside the fire, and above the mantel hung his cherished muskets—each one polished by Catherine's own hands, and, when she was sure no one was watching, fired by her own hand too.

In her lap lay a heavy copy of *Augustine's City of God*, her most recent assignment from Flynn. She had been utterly absorbed, the book balanced precariously on her knees, when the priest's voice broke her concentration.

"Cat—may I have a word?"

Catherine turned quickly, startled from her thoughts. She closed the book and sat up, her expression bright. "Yes, Father?"

Flynn stepped forward slowly, his boots dull against the Turkish rug. He came to stand before the fire, its light flickering across his weary face. He clasped his hands behind his back and said nothing for several seconds. The flames snapped and crackled, impatient for him to speak.

"Catherine," he said at last, his voice heavy with effort, "I'm afraid I've come with very bad news. Your father has died."

The words seemed to hang there like a draft from an open window. Catherine blinked once, then twice, as if trying to shake away a trick of the ear. Her face went white, her lips trembling.

"How?" she whispered. "I saw him last night. Where is he?"

Flynn's eyes softened. "He was murdered, Cat. I was with him when it happened. He's at Dr. Blythe's now. He was poisoned—by someone here in town. Constable Blackwood and Mayor Craig are lookin' into the matter even as we speak."

Catherine's breath caught in her throat. "I need to see him," she gasped suddenly, her voice rising to a plea. "Please—please take me to see Daddy! Please!" The word broke into a cry. "*Pleeeease!*"

Flynn stepped forward, placing a hand on her shoulder. "We'll see him immediately, Cat. I'll have Charles bring your coat and we'll leave at once."

But Catherine was no longer hearing him. She covered her face with both hands, sobbing "Daddy" again and again into her palms. Her body shuddered as the grief took her in waves. Flynn caught her just as her knees began to give. He wrapped his arms around her tightly, letting her cry against his shoulder.

"There now, Cat," he murmured. "It's terrible—absolutely terrible. But I need ye to listen to me for a moment."

Catherine nodded faintly, her sobs slowing to a thin, pitiful sound.

"Good girl," Flynn said softly. "Now sit ye down."

She let him guide her back into the Italian chair. Her eyes were swollen, her cheeks flushed and wet. Flynn crossed to the wet bar, found a decanter, and poured a generous measure of Scotch into a glass.

"Catherine Dryden," he said firmly, returning to her side, "drink this. Right now, please."

Catherine looked up, dazed, still trembling. Flynn held the glass toward her.

"Go on—drink the cup, Cat."

She nodded weakly, raised the glass, and took a small sip.

"No, no," said Flynn, crouching beside her, voice low but insistent. "Big swig now—like an angry sea captain."

Catherine managed a faint, tearful laugh between breaths, then obeyed, taking a long swallow as Flynn rested a hand on her arm, steadying her through the storm.

She drained the glass in one brave swallow, the Scotch burning her throat as it went down. Then she coughed—violently, almost angrily—as if to reject both the liquor and the truth it had been meant to soften. Flynn took the glass from her trembling hands just as a knock came at the door.

Charles entered with her winter overcoat, but he was not alone—behind him came Alice, Catherine's maid since childhood, her eyes already wet. The woman's hands fluttered in agitation as she crossed the room, curtsying awkwardly before hurrying to Catherine's side.

"Oh, my poor lamb," Alice whispered, her voice quavering, "don't stand there in the cold, come now—let me get ye proper." She took up the coat from Charles and began helping Catherine into it, her fingers moving swiftly despite their shaking. Flynn fetched the hat from its peg and handed it over, and Alice set it gently atop Catherine's dark hair, tucking a loose curl behind her ear with the tenderness of a mother.

Catherine stood motionless through it all, letting herself be turned this way and that like a doll being dressed. When Alice buttoned the final clasp, the girl seemed to wake, drawing a shuddering breath.

"You're a Dryden," Alice said suddenly, her voice firming. "You remember that, miss. You've your father's steel in you, you do. The good Lord gives no cross too heavy for a Dryden to bear."

Catherine met her maid's eyes and nodded weakly, tears spilling over again. Flynn placed a steadying hand on her shoulder. "Aye," he said softly. "She's right, Cat. You'll need his strength now."

Together, the three made their way through the great hall of Stratford Hall. The corridors felt unnaturally long, the portraits of ancestors looming overhead, their painted faces grim and knowing. The echo of their footsteps filled the marble passage as if the house itself were mourning.

When they reached the grand staircase, Alice pressed a handkerchief into Catherine's hand. "Keep this, miss," she said. "I stitched it myself, see? A for Alice, but it'll stand for *aid* today."

Catherine gave a watery laugh, clutching the small square of linen to her chest.

At the open door, Mr. Elby was waiting, his hat in hand, his red eyes downcast. The grey morning light cut across the drive, making his tears glisten as Flynn and Catherine approached. He removed his cap and bowed deeply. "I'm so sorry, Lady Catherine—so sorry..." His voice cracked, and he shook his head, overcome. "It's just not right, Lady. Not right."

Catherine's composure crumbled again. "Thank you, Elby," she managed through tears. "Dearest man."

Elby, unable to speak further, opened the carriage door

and helped her inside. Flynn turned to him, gripping his arm. "Good man," he said quietly. "Good man."

The door shut with a soft thud, and Elby climbed to his perch, taking up the reins. With a gentle flick and a muffled command, the horses started forward, their hooves thudding dully against the snow-covered lane.

For several minutes, nothing was said. The carriage swayed and creaked, its interior dim but warm from the small brazier beneath their feet. Catherine stared out through the frosted glass, her tears subsiding into small, rhythmic breaths.

Flynn sat beside her in silence, giving her space to think. He had seen this before—the shift from disbelief to fury. He knew the anger was coming.

And it came. Slowly at first, then rising, fierce and bright.

"Why would he be murdered, Father?" she said suddenly, turning to him with eyes that blazed despite the tears still wet upon her cheeks. "Who would want to murder him? He's never done wrong to anyone—not once in his life!"

Flynn sighed, his breath a mist in the cold air. "That's exactly why, Catherine. Your father was a righteous man—and righteousness breeds envy. Some jealous soul, coveting what he was and what he stood for, has acted foolishly. They'll be found out and brought to justice—mark my words."

Her hands clenched into fists. "How did he die?"

"He was poisoned."

"Was he in pain?"

"I was there," Flynn answered gently. "No, Cat—he wasn't. The poison acted quick, quicker than most would think. He never knew the hand that dealt it."

Catherine turned away again, staring out at the white fields. "Where did this happen?"

"In the carriage, just after we'd left *Ye Olde*."

"When?"

"Last night, around nine o'clock."

She pressed the handkerchief Alice had given her against her lips. "Why didn't you come and tell me sooner?"

"I had Elby take your father straight to Blythe's," Flynn said quietly, his gaze fixed on the snow-frosted fields beyond the carriage window. "I needed the doctor to determine what had happened. For all I knew at the time, he might've suffered a hemorrhage or a stroke—a natural death, perhaps sudden, but not malicious. Yet the swiftness of it—" he shook his head—"it was peculiar. Too quick. And your father was a man of fine health, as strong as an ox and twice as stubborn."

Catherine clutched her coat tighter around her shoulders, her voice barely a whisper. "So you suspected foul play immediately?"

"I did," Flynn replied. "In the meantime, I went to find Isaac Digby. Just before your father collapsed, he'd mentioned that Isaac had been pestering poor William Avondale about young Tildon Allen's death. He believed the two to be connected somehow, though he hadn't said how. He'd suggested we pay Isaac a visit together. So, when he fell ill, I thought it best to continue on to Isaac myself. If your father *had* been poisoned, I reasoned, then it was likely tied to the other deaths."

He paused, drawing a breath, the carriage wheels crunching rhythmically over the snow. "Before returning to the pub, I thought it wise to wait—to give Blythe time to perform his autopsy. Rushing back to Ye Olde might've only spooked the killer—or killers. I'm still uncertain how many may be involved. I've considered the pub a crime scene since last night, and while I haven't yet reached any firm conclusions, what I've found—and what I saw at *The Headless Horseman*—will, I think, cast some light on this murky business."

Catherine looked at him sharply. "*Your* investigation?" she repeated, her brows furrowed. "Father, what if you're murdered as well? You can't go about hunting killers alone. Isn't that Blackwood's duty? And—" she faltered, "—and Whitehouse's?"

Flynn's expression darkened. "Whitehouse is dead too, Cat. Hung from the back of *The Horseman* last night."

Her hand flew to her mouth. "Dear God..."

"Yes," Flynn murmured. "Dear God, indeed. And Blackwood can't manage this on his own. He's competent enough, but everyone in town knows he's half in Levi Bairstow' pocket—and the other half in his pride. He'll need help."

"Then let Mayor Craig and the others handle it!" Catherine pleaded. "You're not a constable, Father. You shouldn't be risking your life."

Flynn gave a low laugh and shook his head. "Your father never shied from a fight. You've never shied from a fight. And the saints know I've never pulled a punch. God forbid we start now." He leaned back, reaching into his coat for his old bent pipe. "Besides, there's fear in the air—thick as fog. Not just of murder, but of ghosts. The dead are said to be walkin', their spirits seen by more than a few."

Catherine shivered, her breath visible in the cold air. "Is this how Diggy comes into the story? Father, bless him, but he's practically an invalid—half daft from loneliness."

Flynn smiled faintly as he tamped the pipe's bowl with his thumb. "Aye, Isaac Digby may be half-mad and fully superstitious—but he's not the only one tellin' ghost tales. Every man at *The Headless Horseman* saw the apparitions together—Allen, Avondale, and Whitehouse, clear as daylight."

Catherine crossed herself instinctively. "Then the devil has come to this town."

Flynn struck a match and lit his pipe, the flame briefly illuminating his weathered face. "I doubt it," he said, puffing once. "He's got grander places to be than the north of England—like the merciless lands of the Mohammedans—to keep their evil burning hot." A wry smile touched his lips as he exhaled a slow ribbon of smoke. "But if he *has* come, my dear, then by God, he'll be cast out."

The carriage lurched over the frozen road, its lanterns throwing pale arcs of light across the snow. Catherine's gloved hands were clenched tight in her lap. Outside, the wind pressed against the glass like a living thing, and the horses' breath rose in clouds of silver steam.

For a long while, neither spoke. The wheels ground over the ruts like distant thunder. Then Catherine broke the silence.

"It couldn't be," she murmured, her voice scarcely audible above the creak of the axles, "that all this—Father's death, the unrest at the mill—is about what I did to Lilly… all those years ago."

Flynn shifted, his heavy coat brushing against the leather seat. "Ah now, Catherine Dryden," he said softly, his voice low but steady, "God doesn't be payin' back evil with evil. You were a child then—frightened, proud, and far too well-kept to know the world as it is. The devil's no claim on ye, an' neither does that poor wee girl."

Catherine's eyes glistened in the half-light. "Then why do I hear her, Flynn? Why do I see her face in the snow outside the Hall? Every Christmas Eve I hear knocking in the east corridor—as if she's still out there waiting to be let in."

Flynn drew a slow breath, the lanternlight flickering across his kind, lined face. "What you're hearin', my dear, isn't the dead—it's your own heart poundin' for mercy. God lets the conscience cry out where the proud once kept silence. That knockin' ye hear—it's not vengeance, love. It's invitation."

Catherine turned toward the window. The landscape rolled past in shades of ash and silver, fields stretching toward the distant spire of Werseby Church. "Then I must make it right," she whispered.

"You will," Flynn said, his tone softening. "An' when ye do, Catherine Dryden, that knockin' will cease—not because the past forgets, but because grace remembers for ye."

TWENTY-ONE

After Catherine had been to Blythe's to see her father's body—laid out cold and colourless beneath a white sheet—something within her shifted. The world had become distant, muffled, like sound through thick glass. She stood beside him longer than anyone thought proper, tracing the line of his jaw with a gloved hand, trying to remember warmth where none remained. When at last Flynn coaxed her away, she walked as one in a dream, her mind sharpening not with clarity but with fury.

At Perely's she chose a coffin without hesitation—the most handsome one in the shop, with brass handles and a lion carved upon the lid. The undertaker, grateful and trembling, spoke of making up a year's wages in a single sale. Catherine didn't care. Money meant nothing; dignity did. Her father had been a man of honour, and honour deserved a noble box. Flynn said nothing. He simply watched her with quiet respect, taking long draws on his pipe, eyes glinting behind the smoke.

Then came the visit to Vicar Johnson, to arrange the service. The irony wasn't lost on Flynn: Lord Dryden had died a loyal Anglican despite decades of Catholic counsel from his resident priest. The old debate returned to Flynn's mind—how many times had he tried to persuade Dryden that the truest Englishman was, by nature, Catholic? But Dryden, firm as oak, had always replied that as the head of a family loyal to the Crown, he must "fall on his sword for King and Country, however perverted the roots of Anglicanism may be," and would quote Rahab the Harlot or Ruth the Moabite as proof that redemption could spring from strange soil.

Catherine knew this speech by heart; she had heard it at table every Michaelmas since she was twelve. Now, reciting it in her mind, she felt the emptiness of it. King and Country had not saved her father. Faith had not saved him. Not even Flynn, with all his holy confidence, had saved him. She felt, for the first time in her life, the terrifying thrill of anger at God.

When the business with the vicar was finished—he had been uncharacteristically gentle, though Flynn suspected he was suppressing a smirk—Catherine and the priest climbed back into the carriage. She was silent for a time, her gloved hands twisting a lace handkerchief to threads. At last she turned to him.

"What now, then?" she asked.

Flynn, bent over his pipe, looked up. "What do you mean, what now?"

"You know *exactly* what I mean." Her voice was hard now, her eyes flashing. "I can practically *smell* that wood-burning intellect of yours, Father. You and that little pocket book—don't think I haven't noticed. I'm not going home to sit by the fire while you get your neck wrung like a chicken."

Flynn couldn't help but laugh. "Come now, Catherine—these things are no joke. T'isn't safe in the town just now. There's more blood and fear about than sense."

She stared straight ahead, jaw set. "Then perhaps it's time someone without sense began asking questions."

Flynn leaned back, puffing his pipe in silence, and thought—*Ah, she's her father's daughter indeed.*

Catherine bent over and produced, from under her seat with a small, decisive flourish, an elaborate hatbox bound with ribbons and seals. She set it on her knees and opened it as if revealing a reliquary.

"You have a new hat to wear, Cat?" Flynn asked, half-smiling despite himself.

She lifted from the box not a hat but a single-shot pistol, cold and brass in the morning light. Calmly, as though arranging gloves, she began to load it.

"Mary and Joseph, Catherine!" Flynn said, startled.

"And Jesus," she added without looking up. "Don't forget Jesus—he'll need to help whoever is responsible for this."

"Catherine—this ain't the Americas—we have law and order," Flynn protested, his voice pitched between a priest's warning and a man's fear.

"Whitehouse himself was killed!" she snapped. "What if Blackwood is in on this? And if it were I who had been poisoned, what would Father have done? Hide at chapel and leave the town to rot? No."

Flynn's hands hovered, helpless. "It is not time for vengeance; it is time for sorrow. This is not the way to mourn. Besides, vengeance does not belong to you—it belongs to God. Nor does the delivery of death belong to you..."

Her eyes flashed. "There will be time for mourning," she said, voice lowering, each sentence polished on intellect as much as on rage. "But now—now I am angry. Angry that the murderer walks. Angry that some brazen thief of life believes he can take my blood with impunity. Angry that I stand, save yourself, entirely alone. What am I to do?

Return home and weep myself into the pillows? I will not."

She straightened and put the pistol back into the box, then closed the lid with the casual quiet of a woman returning a book to a shelf. "I am my father's daughter, Father—Lady Catherine Dryden. This town is part of my stewardship. You have told me that all authority comes from God, and you have taught me that authority is the means by which God ordains peace. My family has kept this place; I am His peace here. If authority must act to preserve life, if the bodies of the poor and honest are being desecrated, then it is not vengeance I seek but protection and, if needs be, the use of force as the law allows."

Flynn's mouth formed an involuntary prayer. "Catherine—listen. Scripture and the fathers, St. Augustine and St. Thomas included, warn against presumption. You speak like a Thomist and so I love you for it, but prudence must temper passion. The moral law—natural law—does allow defence of the innocent. The doctrine of double effect—"

"—Aquinas," she finished. "Yes. I know the doctrine. I was taught how to weigh ends and means. I am not proposing to become judge, jury, and hangman. I am saying that as steward I must act where those charged with the peace fail. If there is a moment when a single shot can stop a killer from spilling another life, then, by God, that shot may preserve life. That principle is not vengeance—it is protection."

Her hands went still in her lap. For a long moment she said nothing, her face drawn tight with thought, the kind of thought that ages a person from the inside out. Then her shoulders dropped, and a strange calm—almost regal—settled over her.

"But I am small," she said quietly, her voice trembling but

clear. "Small, and finite, and bound by dust. There are questions God does not answer—and perhaps cannot be answered by any creature. Job asked *why* and was met not with explanations, but with God Himself. I think I understand that now."

She looked toward the window, where a thin light was beginning to touch the snow. "Anger at God is the sound of a heart still beating—but it's no place to live. I will ask my questions, and then I will be silent. I will remember that I am not the maker of justice, only its servant. And whatever vengeance there is to be had—He will see to it."

Flynn watched her, the priest's face unmasking pride and fear in equal measure. He had taught her the Summa, and now he saw the system turned into armor.

"You've educated a woman, Father," she said more lightly, the old ferocity returning with a smile that did not touch her eyes. "And that is a very dangerous thing."

Flynn stared for a moment, then muttered, "God forgive me," in a voice that was half prayer, half plea. He thrust his head out the carriage window and called to Elby, who sat stiff and waiting on his box. "To Bairstow Textiles, Elby!"

TWENTY-TWO

The Dryden carriage rattled through the cobbled heart of town, its iron rims striking the stones with an uneven clang. They passed *Ye Olde Knights of Jerusalem*, where the Christmas choir's muddled voices carried through the frosted windows—half carol, half cacophony. Flynn craned his neck as they went by, the faint smell of pipe smoke and stout wafting from the doorway. "God bless the carolers," he muttered, not without envy. The thought of a pint and a hymn was nearly too much for the priest after such a day.

They crested the hill and descended the opposite side, where Bairstow & Co. loomed over the street like a black citadel. The sun was lowering fast, bleeding into the rooftops, and the lamplighters were already moving in pairs—thin shadows with torches—kindling the rows of glass lanterns that would burn through the coming snow.

As the carriage slowed, a figure emerged from the factory doors: Mr. Crowley, the manager, his expression sour as vinegar, his coat black as soot, and his cane ticking sharply against the stones. He didn't even glance toward the Dryden carriage, though its lamps were bright and its wheels loud on the street. He simply walked on, head bent, jaw locked, as if he'd rather be anywhere else on earth.

Elby climbed down and swung open the carriage door, but Flynn raised a hand quickly. "Don't make a move," he said in a low voice. Catherine froze, and even Elby stood as still as a statue, hat in hand. Flynn's eyes followed Crowley as he marched down the street and turned at the corner, heading back toward the town square.

"My God," Flynn murmured, barely audible. "So it is."

"What is, Father?" asked Elby.

"It *is* as it *is*, lad! To the bank, Elby—quickly!"

"The bank?" Catherine repeated.

"The bank, Cat! Always to the capital! It's the heart that pumps the poison."

Without hesitation, Elby slammed the carriage door, leapt onto the driver's box, and flicked the reins. The horses sprang forward into a furious trot, the carriage lurching and bouncing over the uneven stones. Inside, Catherine and Flynn were tossed about like dice in a cup.

"That pistol better not go off!" Flynn shouted over the thunder of hooves and wheels.

"I'd never cock a hammer and forget it," she called back, gripping the seat for balance. "I had an excellent teacher."

Flynn laughed, though his eyes stayed sharp as he pointed through the window. "Look there! Crowley's still walking—slow as sin! We'll beat him to it."

Elby turned the corner hard, sparks flying from the wheels. "Close enough!" Flynn barked, and before the carriage had even settled, he flung open the door, jumped to the street, and helped Catherine down. She landed gracefully, skirts flying in the cold wind.

Flynn darted toward the nearest doorway, where a handsome Christmas wreath hung from the brass knocker. Without a moment's pause, he tore it free.

"Father Flynn!" Catherine gasped. "What on earth are you doing?"

"Bringing tidings of great joy," he said, holding it aloft like a trophy.

Catherine frowned. "My father's just been murdered, and I'm dressed in black—it's hardly the season for joy, let alone larceny."

"Aye," Flynn said, adjusting his collar with mock solemnity. "It's a paradox, and the Lord loves a paradox. Now—listen closely. We're here to see the bankers, to change the names on the accounts, and settle the funeral expenses. I'll do the talking. You—keep that pistol in its pretty box. It may be," he glanced down the street toward the factory, "that I don't yet have the right man."

Catherine nodded once, quietly collecting herself, and followed Flynn through the tall oak doors of the Bank. Inside, the lamps were already dimmed for closing, their weak light dancing against the brass fixtures and paneled walls. A single clerk—pale, thin, and prematurely aged by ledgers—looked up from his desk. His nameplate read *Mr. Chutney.*

"The hour grows late, Father Flynn," the clerk murmured, adjusting his spectacles, "and the Bank is about to close for the evening." Then, noticing Catherine's black dress and veil, his expression softened. "My condolences, Lady Dryden—your father was much esteemed here."

Catherine inclined her head graciously.

"Thank you, Mr. Chutney," said Flynn. "We're here to see Mr. John Henry Hill, if he's still in the building."

Chutney nodded gravely and disappeared through a side door. After a short wait, he reappeared and beckoned them through a narrow corridor lined with portraits of unsmiling financiers. They entered a large, dark office smelling faintly of ink and cigar smoke.

"Mr. Hill will be with you shortly," said Chutney before vanishing once more.

Catherine sat down, the hatbox placed neatly on her lap, her gloved hands resting atop it. Flynn began pacing, scanning the titles on the shelves—volumes of *Smith, Mill, Burke,* and *Locke* squeezed shoulder to shoulder between marble bookends. He squinted at a gilded plaque that read *"Kindness is our Capital."*

From the doorway came a deliberate, polished voice. "Lady Catherine."

Catherine looked up. A tall, spare man with silvered hair and the calm, funereal bearing of a banker stepped into the lamplight.

"Mr. Hill," Catherine said, rising slightly.

"My most sincere condolences on the passing of your father," Hill intoned. "Lord Dryden was not only a nobleman of means, but a gentleman of honour."

Catherine sat again and met his gaze steadily. "Thank you, Mr. Hill. It is precisely that honour which brings me here."

Hill moved behind his massive desk, steepling his fingers. "I have already begun the transferral of your father's holdings into your name, my lady. I presume Mr. Perely will soon be calling for funeral funds."

"He will," Catherine replied softly.

"Then—what else may I do for you?"

There was a pause. Flynn's eyes flicked to Catherine.

"Yes," she said clearly. "I'd like to buy the Bairstow factory."

Flynn's hand shot to his temple. *Holy Mother of God,* he thought.

Mr. Hill blinked, then gave a short laugh. "My lady, I hardly think it's for sale—and truth be told, it would be a poor investment for the Dryden estate."

"And why is that, Mr. Hill?" Catherine asked evenly.

Hill clasped his hands behind his back and began to pace. "Because Bairstow is failing. Deliveries behind schedule, accounts in arrears. Between the accidents, the deaths, and the mismanagement of his foremen, the factory is on the brink of default. Should he miss another payment, the Bank itself will own the property. And I fear that will be soon—perhaps within the fortnight."

He sighed, shaking his head. "A pity, too. A great engine of progress reduced to a livery or a warehouse."

Flynn froze. His eyes widened in dawning comprehension. Catherine had done it—without realizing, she had unlocked the very thing he had been chasing. *The capital key.* The poison, the deaths, the ghost stories—it all ran through the Bank.

"I see," Catherine said quietly, the decision falling from her like a bell. "Then I shall purchase it outright—this very estate and the works. Draw up the papers tomorrow, Mr. Hill. I will have the family barrister attend at first light."

Mr. Hill's face changed as though some piece of machinery had slipped within him; colour drained from his cheeks, then bloomed a sour red, the mask of bankerly composure cracking. He folded his hands, then slowly sank into the great leather chair behind his desk, the room seeming to tilt with the weight of his thought. For a long moment he said nothing but breathed shallowly, as if measuring the breath of some unwelcome consequence.

Before anyone could speak, the door opened and Mr. Crowley stepped in, black-gloved and black-coated, his hat in hand. The manager's gaze slid across the room, caught on Catherine for a single second, and he pivoted as if to leave. His retreat was practised—quiet, automatic.

"Oh, Mr. Crowley," Flynn called out softly, holding the note of a man who had just tilted a chessboard. "Could I ask you a question?"

Crowley halted, hesitated, then abandoned his exit. He turned slowly, the leather of his gloves creaking against the cane. He looked at Hill for a flicker of recognition, then returned his attention to Flynn, inscrutable.

Flynn stepped forward, the priest's voice calm yet sharpened by a blade of certainty. "Was it in India with Wellesley that you first learned to tie a garrote?" he asked, carefully, as if gauging a wound. "Fascinatin' skill, that—one remembers Dryden showin' me how the thuggee made such knots. Very soldierly, and rather telling. There are but two men in this town I know who could fashion such a rope—yourself and Dryden."

Crowley's face betrayed nothing. He only leaned upon his cane and stared at Flynn as the priest continued.

"A cunning bit o' workmanship—admirable, really. But the rest of it was clumsy—slapdash, filthy. Cyanide in the cup—too plain, too obvious." Flynn's fingers tapped the leatherbound notebook at his breast. "Dr. Blythe saw it in the black-blue of Dryden's nails the moment the body lay still. That's what gave the hand away."

Catherine lifted the hatbox to her chest and hid her mouth as she began to cry anew. Flynn turned his head away, a priestly distance between grief and proof, then, recovering, he fixed his gaze on the painting that hung above Hill's mantle—an oil of Waterloo, smoke and cavalry and the tilt of history.

"One could have gotten away with simpler murder twenty years hence, before physicians learned to read death's little marks," Flynn murmured. "But when a man who knows about strangling leaves behind a glaring, clumsy tincture—cyanide in the wine—well, it tells its own tale."

A laugh burst from Hill—thin, incredulous, and then full, the sort of sound that does not go with sorrow but with triumph. Crowley turned to look at him in startled disbelief.

"Very, very well done, Flynn," Hill said, the humour like a scalpel. "You have discovered the killer."

Catherine started, rising from her chair. "You claim—" she began, but Hill interrupted with a lifted hand and a smile that did not touch his eyes.

"A nearly flawless performance, Mr. Crowley," Hill purred, addressing the manager. "But the final step remains for me." He reached into the shadowed drawer of his desk and produced, without haste, a single-shot pistol. For a second its metal flashed like a cold eye, then he stood and angled it toward Flynn with a tranquillity that made the room go glassy.

Crowley did not flinch. With a movement smooth as a scabbard's draw, he slipped the crook of his cane and produced a long blade from within the handle—an inward smile of readiness at his lips.

"Father Flynn," Hill said with the utmost civility, "will you join Lady Catherine and take a seat?" His voice was methodical, a registrar ticking entries. "Mr. Crowley, would you be so good as to bring us two glasses of water—and perhaps a couple of cyanide tablets, for form's sake?"

The sentence fell like a bell tolling in a church—an affront so precise it scarcely seemed possible in a place of civility. Catherine's fingers tightened on the hatbox; Flynn's jaw set and his eyes flamed—not with sudden violence but with the cool, inevitable resolve of a man who has been cornered and chooses to stand. The room, once a sanctum of ledgers and polite condolence, had become a theatre of threat. Outside the bank the town's lamplighters moved on, ignorant of the small apocalypse unfolding within.

"Receive the elements."

"I'll take mine with the Glenlivet, if you don't mind, Mr. Hill," Flynn said, the calm of a man who has practiced serenity like prayer. He sat with the deliberate slowness of someone who has already chosen his posture.

Hill's laugh tinkled like cut glass. "Of course, sir. But my real curiosity is directed at the lady—how did you deduce the Bank's hand, Lady Catherine? What little thing gave it away?" He folded his hands behind his back and watched her with the clinical interest of a man reading a balance sheet.

Catherine set the hatbox on her knees as if it were a textbook. Her voice was cool, measured — the voice of someone trained to argue from first principles. "Capital, sir. Always follow the capital." She let the phrase rest a beat. "At first I suspected Bairstow. He's a brutish sort and easy to hate. But I considered gains and losses. Bairstow has everything to lose from these deaths. The Bank alone gains if Bairstow' works fail. If he defaults, the property can be taken for a fraction. That is how your kind thinks of the world — ledgers first, lives as incidental entries."

Hill's smile tightened. "You're audacious, Miss Dryden. Admirable — and dangerous." He shrugged as if to excuse his own appetite for risk. "I did not set out to murder your father, Lady—I truly did not. I admired the man's bearing. But he insisted upon public scrutiny of the factory accounts. He would have undermined the quiet execution of the loan and distracted my stakeholders. I needed the works to fall. Panic moves markets quicker than writs. A little fear—timely calamity—does wonders for a ledger."

Flynn's fingers pressed together on his knee. "And you thought to manufacture terror."

"It is commerce," Hill said simply. "It is not a moral parlour game. One takes the means to an end."

"Why Whitehouse?" Flynn asked, each syllable an attempt to keep the room from spinning.

Hill's eyes narrowed as he explained with a banker's logic. "Whitehouse was theatre. A constable's corpse swings more attention than a private man's illness. Men clutch purses, merchants stop credit lines, and the poor look for scapegoats. Fear is an economy. We engineered distraction so the public eye would not linger on my paperwork."

Catherine's face drained. The hatbox pressed into her palms like a pulse. She said, blunt as a verdict, "You are evil, sir."

Hill's expression shifted but he carried on without blush. "Capital is ugly business, Lady Catherine. The work of empire in India—if you wish to speak of blood, look there. The campaigns, the contracts, the treaties enforced by a sabre—how much of our modern economy was not forged upon such violence? My methods are mild by comparison."

Catherine's answer was immediate and fierce, the academic trained into moral weaponry. "There were Indians who prospered by trade with Britain, and there were those who suffered from the rivalry you speak of. We did not seek conquest for its own sake; we sought partnership in many places. To reduce the history of a great people to excuses for profit now is to miss the moral point entirely. If your hand in empire stains you, it does not license you to stain the streets of Stratford with blood."

The room stilled. Even Crowley, who had returned with two glasses of water — hands trembling a little as he set them down on the desk — looked away. Hill's jaw worked. He had expected grovelling or panic, not the precise rectitude of an argument that cut him at his own premise.

Hill rose slowly then, the pistol still balanced like an accoutrement of his power. He motioned with a narrow nod. "Stand, Father Flynn. Lady Catherine, step forward." His voice was clinical, almost kind. Crowley, with a look that could have been pity, reached into his pocket for the small sachet they had earlier discussed and offered it with a ceremonious care.

Flynn rose, eyes steady, and met Hill without flinching. Catherine's hands tightened on the hatbox; she did not move closer or away. The glass misted in the lamplight, and for a heartbeat the office had the quality of a sacrament.

"My Scotch?" Flynn asked with a quiet, almost amused voice.

"Ah yes." Hill turned, pistol still balanced in his hand, and set it down on the dry bar. He took up the Glenlivet and a glass and began to pour with the slow, deliberate motions of a man who paced his rituals like his ledgers. The amber liquid gleamed like a promise.

Catherine, who had set the hatbox upon the desk, slid the lid aside with a motion practiced and exact. Her fingers found the pistol inside, and without ceremony she cocked the hammer. She rose, took aim, and leveled the small weapon with steady hands at a spot near Hill's back.

A murmur ran through the room like a wind through reeds. Hill heard it, glanced over his shoulder without haste—and then saw her. For a fraction of a breath his face registered surprise, and then amusement returned in a chilling smile.

"Is that a pistol, Lady Dryden?" he asked, leisurely.

"It is a readied pistol, Mr. John Henry Hill," she said, voice like a silver blade.

Hill looked down at the gun on the bar, flicked his gaze back to Catherine, and his smile widened. "Will you take your chances with your pistol," she asked softly, "or will you take your chances with the Crown?"

"I'll take my chances with a woman!" Hill exclaimed, and laughed in a way that fell flat in the room. At once he dropped the Glenlivet—glass smashing—and reached for the pistol on the bar.

At that same moment Crowley moved. Years in service had given the factory manager a practised quickness. He sprang like a coiled thing and swung the blade that had been hidden in the crook of his cane in a long, arcing strike aimed for Flynn's belly.

Catherine's shot cracked. The pistol barked and smoke puffed; the bullet struck Hill in the throat. He staggered back, hands at his windpipe, choking and gurgling as a dark bloom spread over his linen. He went to his knees, fingers clawing futilely at his throat; the sound of his failing breath was a savage, small animal noise.

Flynn, who had not been idle, moved to intercept Crowley. He raised his pipe-hand in reflex to parry, and the blade found his side—sharp, intimate—slicing through cloth and flesh with a hot sting. He cried out once, a sound half-prayer, half-curse, and his fingers closed on Crowley's wrist. Instinct and training braided together; Flynn grabbed, twisted, and drove his other hand up, bringing the heavy crucifix he carried into Crowley's face in a rain of struck wood. Crowley howled, the blade wrenched from its intended arc, but his grip on the handle stayed stubborn. He staggered, dazed, and tried to pull free.

Catherine dropped the empty pistol and darted to Hill's fallen weapon. She seized it, swung, and fired again. The second shot cracked through the room and hit Crowley high on the head. He collapsed in a heap, the blade clattering from his loosened fingers. The force of the impact sent a dark, wet spatter across Flynn's cheek and collar—blood and fragments of bone and tissue—staining his robe. He made a choking sound but did not release his hold, kneeling now, teeth clenched as he pressed his hand to the wound at his side.

Hill's knees hit the carpet. His voice shrank into a rattle, words half-formed and useless. Catherine bent over him, breath shaking with adrenaline and pity both. "I forgive you, Mr. John Henry Hill," she said, unexpected gentleness threaded through steel. “And I pray God forgive you as well. But you cannot live here anymore.”

Hill’s eyes, large and glossy, found hers. For an instant a look like regret—real and small—crossed his face. Then the light dimmed; his head lolled. He made a few indistinct sounds and went still.

Flynn, pale and trembling, let go of Crowley’s wrist at last. He clutched at his side and began to intone, quiet and steady, prayers in Latin—an ordered litany in the face of chaos, fingers slick with blood. His voice trembled but did not break.

The door burst open. Chutney and two clerks tumbled into the office, faces of ledger-paper shock. The glass-strewn floor and the two men prostrate in blood met their eyes.

“What the devil is going on here?” Chutney demanded, voice high and incredulous.

“Send for Constable Blackwood, Dr. Blythe, and Perely,” Catherine answered, her voice now the iron of command. She straightened, placed Hill’s pistol gently on the desk, and looked down at Flynn. “Father, remain with Mr. Crowley. I will await the constable with Dr. Blythe and Perely. We will not leave this room until law arrives.”

Chutney fumbled for his hat. Outside, the street resumed its indifferent murmur, but the bank’s office sat frozen, lamplight and spilled whisky and a scent of gunpowder lingering like a new truth.

TWENTY-THREE

That same evening the whole town seemed to squeeze itself into the two great inns—news travels faster than sleet when there's blood on the road—and folk scurried from door to door, breath puffing like steam, to trade the latest details of the morning's drama. By dusk both *Ye Olde Knights of Jerusalem* and *The Headless Horseman* were full to their rafters: some came for curiosity, some for consolation, and some because the idea that the killer had been shot felt, perversely, like warming by a hearth.

Constable Blackwood had been thorough; after a brief interview with Lady Catherine and Father Flynn, after an examination of the officer and of Crowley's fallen form, and after the collection of papers and the small, damning things that men drop when they mean to murder—letters, ledgers, receipts—he pronounced, with a voice almost embarrassed by its own certainty, that Flynn and Catherine were "heroes indeed." The room answered him with a baffled cheer; it was as though the town, starved for moral clarity, had been given it in a lump.

Dr. Blythe had bandaged Flynn's side in the corner of Perely's back room with the brisk competence of a man used to the theatre of death. He wrapped the priest in layers of linen and told him, in no uncertain terms, to rest. Flynn complained that the carriage back to Stratford Hall might jar the wound, that sitting was the most unnatural of things for a priest on a night like this, and, with a grin that belied the pain beneath, suggested they take a little refreshment at *Ye Olde* to "ease the pain of a carriage jostle." Catherine, whose nerves had gone from rage to exhaustion and now to the brittle amusement that follows a blow, agreed.

They were given the place of honor—the mayor's table, a privilege that both embarrassed and amused them. The fire at *Ye Olde* burned brighter than usual; the smell of wet coats and burnt ale and a hundred hands clapping rubbed at everyone's sleeves. People clustered round, leaning in as if proximity conferred ownership of the story. Questions tumbled one atop another—Who fired first? Who gave the order? Did Lady Catherine truly aim?—and Flynn ate them like bites of something sharp, answering with a priest's candor and a raconteur's timing.

Mayor Craig, flushed with civic triumph, lifted a glass and called for a toast to God, the town, and the Dryden name. Glasses rose and fell, a muffled roll of approval. Men slapped Flynn on the back. Women dabbed at their eyes. Perely, who had supplied coffins and sympathy in equal measure, hovered near the doorway with his hands folded like a man ready to invoice.

Into this warm, noisy fold came Levi Jonathan Bairstow, flanked by the Hedge brothers—Sam's fresh bruise still tender—and the pub's buzz dimmed into a hush as he stood before the mayor's table. Levi wiped his mouth on the back of a hand and spoke in that blunt, ragged cadence that the town had long learned to take at face value.

"Lady Catherine," he began, "I don't rightly know how to say this proper, but I owe ye everyfing. Ye saved the factory—an' you saved, maybe, me own skin. I ain't proud of how I was wiv yer dead father—he done me wrong a' times, 's true. But I was wrong to think he was the devil in the details. Sometimes the man you reckon is yer enemy's only confused friend, an' the one you think a friend is the snake under yer bed. Me and Flynn—we owe ye both a debt that's big as God's own bell. Thank ye—an' Merry Christmas to ye."

"To Father Flynn and Lady Dryden," said Levi, lifting his glass above the press of shoulders and heads.

"To Father Flynn and Lady Dryden!" the room answered, a dozen voices crashing together as mugs cleared and a long swallow of ale chased the smoke out of many throats.

"Mr. Bairstow," Catherine said simply, standing. The hush tightened like a drawing-room curtain, every face turned toward her—men still smelling of soot and gunpowder, women with handkerchiefs at their mouths, the Privateers clustered by the hearth like a pack of small, raucous sheep. The hatbox sat on her knee, its ribbons untied but its contents, for the moment, unneeded.

"As you men know," she began, voice steady though the tremor beneath it showed, "my father always cared for this town—not for its ledgers alone, nor for what any of you did for us, but for you, your kin, and your lives." She looked to Levi, then to Sam Hedge, to Mayor Craig and, with a quick glance that made several men flinch, to Constable Blackwood. "Any quarrel he had with some of you was because he cared how the poor and the weak were treated. His zeal sometimes read as harshness. For that, if any here felt wronged, he would be the first to ask forgiveness."

A murmur ran through the room; someone said, "Aye," under their breath. Catherine lifted a hand, palm out, stilling the sound.

"Tonight—on this most strange Christmas Eve—I ask of you this: join me. Join the Drydens—if not by name, then by covenant." She set the hatbox beside her and leaned forward. "We may sit apart by birth and station, but this family's duty is stewardship. To keep this town a home. As a steward, I will not let it be ground down by cold accountancy or by fear. I pass my father's mantle to you—the mantle of care, of protection, of responsibility."

She moved through the images as if they were threads in a tapestry she was undoing and reweaving. "Sometimes that mantle will require grief," she said quietly. "Sometimes it will require charity. Tonight it required a musket ball—God forgive us—because it was that or watch more lives be taken. Tomorrow it may mean hanging a wreath on a door. The day after, leaving bread in a child's hand. The Drydens have minded this town for generations. If we fail now, what has all that meant?"

Someone in the back breathed, "Amen," and a woman dabbed at her eyes. Father Flynn's jaw worked; a wet bead ran slow down his cheek and he wiped it not with a handkerchief but with the back of his knuckle as if embarrassed to be human in public.

Catherine's throat tightened. "I do not ask you for blind loyalty. I ask that you share stewardship—share in the keeping of law and charity, and in the hard things that follow. If any of you would refuse this charge, stand now and say so. But if you accept—if you accept right care for the weak, a fair wage, and a town that will not be bullied by ledger or by fear—then raise your glass."

Mugs went up slowly at first, then with gathering force. Billy and the Privateers stamped and whooped. Old Thom's rag scraped faster on a glass. Even the men who'd cursed the

Drydens in darker hours lifted their mugs, some with tears in the corners of their eyes, some with a hard, new look of resolve.

"To the happiest Christmas," said Catherine, voice now a clear bell in the room.

"To the happiest Christmas!" they shouted back, and the sound rolled out through *Ye Olde Knights of Jerusalem* like a benediction—half prayer, half promise—while outside the snow fell silent and clean as a white page laid down for what might come next.

TWENTY-FOUR

Cacophony had reigned at *The Headless Horseman* all evening—the sort of rough music that the working poor make when they let relief leak out of their ribs. Dicky Kimble, who'd decided that the banker's death warranted a celebration, had fetched his battered fiddle—affectionately named "Hussy"—and scraped at a dozen old reels with the concentrated gusto of a man who'd never learned the difference between grace and gusto. The Privateers howled like a pack of young hounds at the bar; Dicky fiddled on, all elbows and grin, and the room rocked with a drunken, ragged joy.

Halfway through a fourth, stumbling rendition of *Greensleeves*, a sudden wind slammed into the low rafters as if a door to the sky had been opened. Every lantern guttered and went out in a single, breathless instant—flames snuffed as though someone had drawn a dark hand across them—save for the hearth, whose logs suddenly flamed a weird, white heat, spitting sparks high into the smoky air. The men's singing cut off mid-phrase; mugs hung halfway to mouths. Something like a chill ran through the crowd: many had seen such a dark trick before, and knew how quickly the uncanny could turn a room.

From the mouths of extinguished candles the smoke rose and gathered, gathering into itself like a congregation, until it took shape. Four bodies of pale, blue light formed in the centre of the floor, hovering just above the grain of the boards: Tildon

Allen, small and translucent as a boy; William Avondale, gaunt and sorrowful; Philip Whitehouse, his constable grin pulled into a rictus; and Lord Dryden, grander even in death, blue as the ghost of a flag. They were no thicker than steam, yet each held the unmistakable outline of a life lately lived—hair, boots, the fold of collars—flickering with the smoke.

The four spoke at once, voices like air over ice, long sibilant notes that wrapped the rafters. "Haaaaaast thooou fouuuuund ouuuuur juuuuuussssstiiiiicccce?" they asked, mournful and unhurried.

Henry, who had been leaning on the bar as if the world might tumble and he could hold it, answered rapidly for the crowd before anyone else could find words. "The men who did it were found and killed," he shouted, voice clear. "They were John Henry Hill and his aid, Crowley—your daughter, Lady Catherine, and Father Flynn did what needed be done. Have ye not seen them where ye are?" His words were a salve and an accusation wrapped together.

The ghosts released a wail that cut like a hawk's cry, thin and terrible. For a moment every man in the room felt his own skin pull tight. Dryden's ghost murmured with a hymn-like sorrow, "Wheeeeeere weeeeeee arrrrrre, theyyyyyyy arrrrrre nooooot." There was a mournful finality to it, as if a footstep had been closed behind some invisible door.

Whitehouse's voice drifted like incense: "Weeee rreeeeeeesssstt innnnnn puuuuuriiiifiiiiicaaaaaattttionnnn." The men nearest to the hearth crossed themselves with fingers that shook; a few muttered hurried prayers without thinking.

Avondale's ghost leaned in as if to peer at the startled faces and asked, the vowels drawn thin, "Thennnnn the tooooow-wwwn isssssss saaaaaaafe?" His question held more fear than would a living man's, more hope than grief.

"Yes, William—the town is saved," Henry answered again, firm now, as if to close the account, "But why now? Why at all? Is there any rhyme to your haunting?"

"Avondale's ghost replied, "Theeeeee hoooooourrr oooooffff Chriiiiiiiisssttssss biiiiiiiiiiirthhhhh iiiiiiiisssss thhhheeeeeeee hoooooooouurrrr oooooffff meeeeeerrccyyyyy aaaaaannnddd trrruuuuuuuuthhhhh..."

Tildon, the boy-ghost, breathed out a single, pure note that might have been a laugh or a blessing: "Peeeeeeeace haaaaas coooooome. Thaaaaaank the Sssssspiiiiirrriiiit."

"Aaaaaaaameeeennn," the four intoned together, and with that the blue lights unstitched themselves from the smoke and rose like a handful of ash up through the rafters. They slipped between tiles and through the thatch, vanishing into the winter sky. For a beat the pub was swallowed in silence so complete that a pinfall would have been indecent.

Henry was the first to move, the kind of man for whom action is prayer. He bellowed, plain and warm, "They've gone—and that's probably that!" His voice was half relief, half dare.

A score of other sounds broke the hush: a glass rattled, someone's knees cracked as he rose, and then a strange, choking noise—the Privateers laughing, incredulous and loud, as if to ward off the terror with noise. Dicky, who had been poised to resume his fiddling, jabbed a finger at a man who had earlier mocked the whole affair and roared, "I told ya, ya filthy pagan!" The insult landed with the fermented sweetness of a town reclaiming a story that had been spun from the edge of fear into a yarn of communal salvation.

TWENTY-FIVE

Spring leaned in slow and sure, and Werseby mended itself in small, unmistakable ways. Lady Catherine set the factory's ledgers right, insisted on fair wages, put Perely and trusted foremen in charge of repairs, and opened a small fund so the Privateers might eat and learn a trade. Orders increased—merchants preferred honest cloth—and the mill, under new stewardship, hummed for the town rather than against it.

Father Flynn walked the lanes like a kindly sentinel: visiting beds, saying Mass for the grieving at St. George's, delivering funerals with a steadier hand, and listening at doors where men at last spoke their fears aloud. He taught catechism to the factory boys and read the dying their final prayers with the same rough tenderness he'd given them in life.

The Bank—sharp and embarrassed—sent a formal apology, published in ink and read aloud at the assembly: condolences from deceased managers and a pledge that the Bank would underwrite reforms, lest profit again be placed above people. It was a small thing, and precisely the sort of thing Catherine required.

Before Easter, Catherine raised a memorial at the edge of the Dryden estate—a simple stone, unmarked save for the carving of a small doll above the words: *Lilly Cooper, Child of God, Remembered.* Each Christmas thereafter, the townsfolk laid holly and candles there, and Catherine herself would kneel by the stone in silence. The snow always fell gently in that spot, never drifting too high, as if heaven itself held its breath.

In time, the knocking at Stratford Hall ceased. Catherine came to believe, as Flynn had told her, that ghosts came only at Christmas because the living remembered least then—the season when joy made them careless, and grace had to come knocking to be let in. It was not the dead who haunted the living, but the living who haunted their own unrepented mercies.

Diggy and his sheep, Bubs, moved into a little cottage on Dryden land under Catherine's care. She watched Diggy grow calmer; Bubs grew fat and famous for the ribbons Flynn tied to his fleece. They lived out their days safe, visiting the pubs as honoured curiosities, and when at last they passed—one after the other—Catherine saw them buried with the same care she'd demanded for every soul in Stratford Hall: a cross and wreath upon the hill, and the whole town in attendance.

And each Christmas Eve, as the bells of St. George's rang clear across the snowbound roofs of Werseby, Catherine would pause by the great door of the Hall and listen. The wind would sigh against the panels, but no knock ever came again.

www.ingramcontent.com/pod-product-compliance
Lightning Source LLC
Chambersburg PA
CBHW010745310726
48980CB00004B/372

* 9 7 9 8 9 9 3 8 4 3 1 0 0 *